Chasing Rumi

Chasing Rumi

A Fable

About Finding

the Heart's

True Desire

Roger Housden

HarperSanFrancisco
A Division of HarperCollins*Publishers*

The Rumi poems in this book were rendered into English by the poet, Coleman Barks. Barks is the author of a number of best selling versions of Rumi poetry, including *The Essential Rumi* and *The Soul of Rumi,* both published by Harper San Francisco.

Grateful acknowledgement is made to Coleman Barks for the following permission to reprint previously published material.

"Love Dogs" from The Essential Rumi, translated by Coleman Barks with John Moyne, HarperSanFrancisco, copyright © 1995 Coleman Barks. "Feeling the Shoulder of the Lion" from Say I Am You: Poetry Interspersed with Stories of Rumi and Shams by John Moyne and Coleman Barks, Maypop Books, Copyright © 1994 Coleman Barks.

HarperCollins books may be purchased for educational, business, or sales promotional use. For information please write: Special Markets Department, HarperCollins Publishers, Inc., 10 East 53rd Street, New York, NY 10022.

HarperCollins Web site: http://www.harpercollins.com

FIRST EDITION

Library of Congress Cataloging-in-Publication Data

Housden, Roger
Chasing Rumi : a story about finding the heart's desire /
Roger Housden.
p. cm.
ISBN 0-06-008445-6
1. Jalâl al-Dân Râmâ, Maulana, 1207–1273—Appreciation—Fiction.
I. Title.
PS3608.086 C47 2002
813'.6—DC21 2002190229

Book Design by Ralph Fowler

Illustrations by Kathleen Edwards after Sandro Botticelli, "The Birth of Venus," c. 1485–86

02 03 04 05 06 ❖RRD(H) 10 9 8 7 6 5 4 3 2 1

1948

GEORGIOU ran lightly, two steps at a time, up the worn marble stairs that lead to the Museo San Marco in Florence. It was an afternoon of steady light in the summer of his eighteenth year. At the top of the stairs he paused for a moment, aware suddenly of that museum flavor—the high, arched ceilings, the faint odor of polish from a dark wooden floor, the cool touch of the handrail, a brass one, that accompanied the stairs. The museum had once been a monastery, and in the fifteenth century Fra Angelico, the great Renaissance painter, had been a monk there. One of his duties had been to adorn each of the monks' cells with a fresco.

When Georgiou turned to face the entrance to the monks' dormitory, his eyes met the glow of a delicate radiance. Through the open archway, like an apparition, *The Annunciation,* Fra Angelico's masterpiece, shone down on him from a large stone wall. In seconds, his natural exuberance gave way to a mood more sober and thoughtful. Something in the flowing grace of the angel Gabriel's robe—or perhaps it was the reverence the angel and the Virgin showed in inclining toward each other—checked his youthful step and drew his attention inward.

A few moments there at the top of the stairs, and he started along the corridor, moving slowly now. He peered round the first couple of arched doors into the small, whitewashed rooms, pausing briefly to take in the frescoes that the master had painted for the monks' contemplation. When he came to the next door, he stepped inside the cell.

There, painted directly onto the dry surface of the wall, was the fresco depicting the Sermon on the Mount. The disciples were gathered in contemplation round Jesus. He was sitting a little above them on a stylized rock washed in a soft yellow that glowed on the wall of the cell. Christ's right arm was raised, his forefinger pointing to heaven.

Georgiou stood in front of the painting entranced—by the luminous tones, lavender and green, of the disciples' robes, the remarkable simplicity of the drawing, but above all by the look on the faces of the disciples. They were filled with a rapture he had never known existed; a tangible sweetness of love, which was both of this world and not of it at the same time. Their expression seemed to show a love for Jesus, the man, and also for something else that could never be put into words. His legs began to tremble, his back turned cold.

The thoughts in Georgiou's mind ebbed away. Unable to take his eyes from those beautiful faces, he fell into a deep silence. His strength failed him, and he sank slowly to the floor. How long he sat there, lost in the masterpiece, he had no idea. When he finally got to his feet he knew, though not with his ordinary mind, that he had been filled with the love that makes the world.

1958

2

FLORENCE: the name lingers on the tongue like the taste of fine wine. It was only the night before that his friend Andros had mentioned its meaning—the city amid the flowers. Now, in the fresh light of morning, Georgiou strolled through the Colonnade of the Innocents, the masterpiece that Brunelleschi—the same Brunelleschi who built the dome of the city's great cathedral—had conceived some six centuries before for the façade of the city orphanage.

He glanced up between the arches of the Colonnade and took in, as he had done many times before, the exquisite medallions of babes in swaddling clothes. He stopped to gaze in the window of a shop selling marbled papers. A newspaper vendor was calling out the morning's headlines. Housewives—their hands doing most of the talking—were haggling with the fruit and vegetable sellers under the Colonnade's arches.

A tall young woman was strolling a few yards ahead of him. He took in her long fair hair, the sway of her floral dress. A tourist, no doubt, the season beginning already. He crossed the piazza to the Caffè Bergelli, sat on the *terrazza,* and ordered a cappuccino. With his cup raised to his lips, he watched the flower sellers in the piazza setting their blooms in order; arranging peonies and camellias in their different colors, shades of red and white; placing lilies and roses in vases according to the length of their stems.

Sunlight was already streaming into the square, the Piazza of the Blessed Annunciation. In its center the statue of Duke Ferdinand stood, and for a moment, the duke's solemn head shone gold. Young women, their long black hair flicked by the wind, click-clacked past Georgiou's table on their way to work. Lambrettas scooted around the corner of the Via Battisti, filling the piazza with the whining of oversized gnats. The year was 1958. Then, as always, the rest of the world beat a path to Florence.

Ruth Orkin, the famous American photographer, had recently captured the spirit of the city's street life for the world. Her lens had found a café full of Italian stallions turning to look at a single passerby, a demure young woman who kept her eyes in front of her, a faint smile on her lips. The eternal dance, with no clear indication of who was in charge. Italy was rising and vibrant again, the horrors of war already fading into memory.

3

LIKE MANY young men, Georgiou enjoyed the banter of café life, though he was a little shy and retiring in the company of women. While most of his peers stayed late in those same cafés, Georgiou would often leave early and go to the churches and museums, spending hours there gazing upon the city's great works of art.

The one place he avoided was the Museo San Marco. For never again—though he had gone back to that cell several times—did he have the vision of beauty that had poured through his veins the first time he saw Fra Angelico's fresco of the Sermon on the Mount. It was some years ago now that he had decided his loss of vision would be easier to bear if he no longer returned to the scene.

Perhaps it was that loss of something once fleetingly known that rubbed away at his soul like a grain of sand; that impelled him to throw himself into his painting and into his thirst for wild adventures. Georgiou was a fine icon painter. He had been schooled in the art by his father, Stefanou, who had come to Italy from Greece before the war to seek a better life for himself and his family. His wife had died on the journey, and when the Greek finally settled in Florence to continue his art, he raised his son on his own.

Florence had been kind to Stefanou and his son. The Greek community there was small, and not many people had need of an icon. But there were plenty who needed a good restorer of old paintings, and the Greek and his son had become respected in the town for their art and skill. Their needs were few and they lived simply, in a tiny apartment on a cobbled street near the Museo San Marco, a few moments away from the Caffè Bergelli.

For a lover of beauty, of art, of ideas, such as Georgiou, there were few better places to be than the city he lived in. Yet from time to time, and for years now, a strange melancholy, a dissatisfaction, would come over him, and in this mood the fine light of Florence became oppressive to the young painter.

When the restlessness began to stir in his chest, Georgiou would start walking. He would walk, not to the local piazza, not even up into the hills of Fiesole above the city. No, his thirst was far bigger, far wilder than that. Already, in his twenty-eight years, he had set off for places with names like Sarajevo, Skopje, and Krakow, in Poland. To places whose names jumped out at him from the atlas. Once, he went to the Greek Orthodox monastery of Saint Catherine's, in the Sinai desert of Egypt. Another time, he traveled all the way to Kiev, in the Ukraine. Georgiou loved the atlas more than any other book. He loved to pore over the continents and trace a line with his finger along a great river, over a desert, along the Mediterranean coast of North Africa, or a mountain range.

"That's where I'll go," he would say, when he could restrain his yearning no longer. And unlike most people, he usually did.

When he reached the pitch of intensity at which he felt he must free the wildness in his veins or suffocate in the civilized air of Florence, he would give notice to his father of his plan for a journey. His father was a wise and simple man, not given to making his son in his own image. Though he did not understand his son's urges, Stefanou invariably gave him his blessing. He knew that his son was both blessed and cursed with a questioning mind. The puzzles of life—why we are born, what happens at death—seemed to cling like an adder to Georgiou's young and gifted heart.

"I have a philosopher for a son," he would say to his friends, partly by way of excuse, but not without a hint of pride. "What can you do with such a one? He has all he could wish for here, but he longs for something else that he cannot even put into words, just like his mother before him. He will never be content to stay in one place with one thing. I don't know what will become of him."

So it was that, a few weeks after his finger had traced its passage over the atlas and inscribed a route or a name in his imagination, Georgiou would be there, his questions hoping for answers in fresh terrain.

Yet for a year or more now—ever since he returned from his last journey—Georgiou had begun to feel differently about traveling, and even about his own questions. He felt that this fire in his breast would never be cooled by anything. Neither travel nor colorful experiences seemed to dampen its embers for long. Better to follow the advice of his father, he thought, and appreciate the gifts of his life in Florence than to run everywhere looking for something he had no name for. And that, for a year and a day, is exactly what he had done.

4

GEORGIOU took out the slim volume of poetry that Andros had given him the night before and laid it on the table. The *terrazza* was filling with the first batch of onlookers and cappuccino lovers of the day.

Though Georgiou had friends his own age, his closest friend was Andros, who was a little younger than Georgiou's father. Andros was also Greek. Despite his age, he still had a shock of unruly black hair, and the strong presence of a man who was at home in the world. He was the one person who seemed to understand Georgiou's urge to travel. Andros laughed easily and liked to sit in the cafés in the Piazza San Marco and watch the day go by. Yet he, too, had spent much of his youth traveling with questions on his mind. He reflected deeply on life, and often spent long periods alone. Something of a philosopher, Andros was always reading books by people who had lived a long time ago—like Dante, Plato, Euripides, and others with names that Georgiou could barely pronounce.

Georgiou had stopped by his house the previous night, and Andros had noticed that his young friend seemed quieter than usual. Raising his thick eyebrows, Andros turned his large brown eyes to Georgiou and said,

"Is there no call for an icon painter this spring, or is there something that weighs on you more heavily than the concerns of making a living?"

Georgiou smiled at his friend's gentle way, so familiar to him now, of drawing him out.

"Life is good, Andros," Georgiou began. "I live in one of the most beautiful cities in the world, I love my work, and we have enough clients. Whenever I have dreamed of setting out on an adventure, my father has given his blessing, and I have gone where I wanted. How is it, then, that I still have a wish, like some yeast fermenting beneath my skin, for something I cannot quite name? However good life appears to be, nothing ever seems to fill this gap. I think my legs have grown heavy and tired of seeking answers. I seem to have been looking in all the wrong places. I have come to think that I should learn to be happy with what I have here in Florence. Or maybe it is more than that. I am beginning to think my task is to learn to be happy with who I am."

Andros listened carefully.

"Maybe so," he said, after a moment's pause. "Maybe so. It is true that your life here in Florence is blessed with good fortune. Yet I hear more than a hint of resignation in your voice. You seem to feel you should count your blessings and be thankful for the life you have; that you should forget this feeling of lack that persists despite your good fortune. But no one can make themselves into what they are not, Georgiou. Why not be thankful for what you have *and* listen to what your sorrow is telling you? This yearning that afflicts you is a special kind of suffering, my friend, and suffering can become its own cure. Have you heard of the poet Rumi?"

Georgiou shook his head.

Andros took down a slim volume from his bookshelves. "Jelaluddin Rumi lived in the city of Konya, in Turkey, in the thirteenth century. He was the founder of the mystical sect of Muslims known as the Whirling Dervishes, which still exists to this day. He was also a great poet. Perhaps this poem will remind you of someone you know."

Andros started to read out loud:

Last night a man was crying, Allah! Allah!
His lips grew sweet with the praising.
Until a cynic said,
So! I've heard you
calling out, but have you ever
gotten any response?
The man had no answer to that.
He quit praying, and fell into a confused sleep.

He dreamed he saw Khidr, the guide of souls,
In a thick green foliage.
Why did you stop praising?
Because I never heard anything back.
This longing you express is the return message.
The grief you cry out from
Draws you to union.
Your pure sadness
That wants help
Is the secret cup.
Listen to the moan of a dog for its master.
That whining is the connection.
There are love dogs
No one knows the names of.
Give your life to be
One of them.

Georgiou sat for some moments with his chin cupped in his hands. "But Andros," he said finally, "how do you give your life to something you don't even understand?"

"Your longing cannot be remedied by strategies," Andros replied. "All you can do is to follow your heart's prompting. This feeling is a gift, Georgiou. When it comes over us, we must watch it, and not let our ordinary minds get in the way. The feeling itself is authentic. It shows you are close to something. We don't really feel deprived until we are close."

The older man put a hand on his young friend's shoulder. "All shall be well, Georgiou," he said, his eyes warm and reassuring. "All is already well. Listen to what your heart tells you, and you cannot stray far."

Andros placed the book of poetry in Georgiou's hands. "Why not take this home with you this evening," he said. "You may find it speaks to you in other ways. When you are on your own, open the book at random, and see what you find on the page."

5

GEORGIOU had not taken the book out of his pocket since the night before. But as he sat on the Bergelli *terrazza* watching the world go by, he could still feel the echoes of his conversation with Andros. He felt humbled, chastened somehow, by what his friend had read him. Reassured, too, that he was not wrong for feeling the way he did. He finished his coffee, his eyes resting on nothing in particular. Then he remembered Andros's suggestion. He let the volume fall open and propped it against his coffee cup. His eyes fell upon these few lines:

All the particles of the world
Are in love and looking for lovers.
Pieces of straw tremble
In the presence of amber.

He read the lines twice, then slowly put the book down flat on the table. A shudder of cold passed over him, though the morning was already warm. Rumi's words reached down into him and touched a tenderness beyond all his questioning, beyond all his ardor and desire for life. Tears began to well in his eyes. This poet, a stranger, knew him by heart.

Why were these lines so painful, such a relief, so bitter and sweet? Never in his twenty-eight years had Georgiou known such a trembling as that reading brought upon him. Never, except for the first time he had gone to the Museo San Marco.

Georgiou sat there for a long time, barely aware of the world around him. Something was stirring in him. Georgiou knew, but in a way that was softer, gentler, than the surfeit of energy that had prompted his adventures so far, that he had to go to the place where Rumi had written this poem.

He would go this time not as an adventurer, not as a curious traveler. Nor would he go because he didn't know what else to do. He would go because of that trembling. He would go because his heart said so, without needing the words to say why.

6

THERE WAS no reason to wait; Georgiou decided to leave the very next day. He hurried home to tell his father and to set his affairs in order. That same evening, he went to bid farewell to Andros.

Andros sat the young man down at his oak table and placed before him a bowl of white bean soup, some dark bread, and a glass of dry white Chianti. He glanced at Georgiou's bag by the door and, with a benevolent smile, asked him the question that by now had become a familiar refrain between them.

"Where is it this time, my friend?"

"Konya," Georgiou replied.

Andros nodded and smiled.

"Which poem was it?" he asked.

Georgiou told him about the poem and his trembling. Andros listened, and looked at him for a long time before speaking.

"This journey may be your undoing," he said finally. "You would be wise to reflect carefully on your true motives for such a pilgrimage, Georgiou. Konya has been a place of no return for many, including Rumi."

"I don't have a motive, a reason for going," Georgiou replied. "I only know I must go where that trembling takes me. My life will mean nothing if I don't."

Then Georgiou looked up at his friend.

"But what do you mean," he went on, "when you say that Konya was a place of no return for Rumi?"

"It was there that he died into love," Andros replied. "His poems are his ashes. He met his teacher, Shams, in Konya. Shams knew of Rumi's reputation as a famous scholar and theologian. He traveled to Konya, marched into Rumi's study, threw his books out the window, and told him there was no love, no truth, that did not exist in this fleeting moment. Rumi would not find God in books, in sophisticated theories, or in the afterlife; that was all fantasy, Shams had roared. He would find Him now, in this world, or not at all. From that moment on, Rumi and Shams shared a love that encompassed both worlds, the human and the divine. When Shams was murdered out of jealousy by Rumi's students, Rumi fell utterly into the madness of grief and love. It is from that divine madness that his poems were born.

"Konya is a destination for lovers," Andros went on. "That is why I say it is dangerous. This time you are setting out on a real journey, Georgiou, and I am sure you will receive exactly what your soul requires. No more and no less. I want to give you two pieces of advice. First, in every situation you meet on the way, be sure to tell the absolute truth as you know it. Second, pay attention to your dreams. If you do these two things, your way will be smoothed from the very beginning."

Andros opened the drawer in his desk and handed Georgiou two sealed letters.

"When you left with Rumi's poetry last night, I knew you would go to Konya," he smiled. "I have written two letters of introduction for you. There are two friends of mine that I would wish you to meet on the way. One is my brother, Father Dimitri, who lives in the monastery of Iveron on the Holy Mount Athos. He has painted icons all his life, and has a deep love for the Virgin Mary. Then there is Hassan Shushud in Istanbul. Hassan is a mystic who is respected by all the different sects of Muslim dervishes. He will certainly give you help on your journey."

"You know me better than I do myself," laughed Georgiou, as he slipped the letters into his bag. They spoke on for a while, capping the white wine with a couple of Greek ouzos, until finally they embraced and Georgiou stepped out into the cool of the night. As he passed through the Piazza San Marco, a few late drinkers were still swapping tales in the cafés. But Georgiou didn't notice them. He was already between worlds, like a goat in midair between two crags.

7

GEORGIOU set out early the next morning while most of the city was still sleeping. He walked through the narrow streets and down the Via San Giuseppe to the magnificent Church of Santa Croce, where tourists streamed daily to visit the tombs of Michelangelo and Galileo. Outside the church was a towering statue of Dante. Georgiou looked up for a moment at the face of the city's greatest poet of love, then bent his head and silently asked for Dante's blessing.

Then he was off, down past the Leather School, crossing the River Arno by the Ponte Santa Trinita, and along the Via Carmina to the bus station. There he would find a ride to Brindisi, the port from which boats left for the coast of Attica. The pigeons were just waking on the ledges of the Duomo, the street cleaners were washing down the piazzas, the bakers were stoking their ovens, the flower sellers were unloading their blooms in the market. Florence was making ready for another light-filled day.

8

WHEN HE STEPPED ashore from the overnight mail boat onto the Greek mainland beyond the island of Corfu, Georgiou found a truck driver in a café who offered to take him to a place called Meteora, halfway to the city of Thessaloníki and the Holy Mountain of Athos. Through forests of pine, through mountains and valleys of black rock and wild thyme they drove, until finally Georgiou stepped down from the truck in the upper valley of a rushing river.

Never had he seen such a strange place. There, in the midst of a broad plain, natural formations of rock towered thousands of feet above the valley floor, like the fingers of some buried giant's hand. On the summit of each of the rock towers was an ancient monastery. An evening mist swirled around these, the monasteries of Meteora. Making his way to the base of the pinnacle that seemed to hold the largest monastery, Georgiou began climbing the hundreds of steps that wound round the rock tower to the buildings at the top.

So it was that Georgiou found himself knocking at the thick wooden door of Megalo Meteora, the Monastery of Transfiguration, the largest and most ancient monastery in all of Greece, in the wild and mountainous hinterland, the home of his forebears.

It was a few moments before the door opened, and then only a crack. A gruff voice asked his business.

"A room for the night," Georgiou replied.

"Not possible. Feast of Saint John Chrysostom," the voice replied. The door snapped shut.

Georgiou banged again, shouting that he had nowhere else to go, that he had come a long way, all the way from Florence in Italy, and that this was no way to treat a poor traveler in the land of his forebears. The door opened a crack again.

"Are you Orthodox?" the voice asked.

"Yes, I am; and a painter of icons," Georgiou replied.

The door opened wide, and a stooped old man with a long gray beard and black habit ushered him in. He led Georgiou to the guest master, who showed him to a room on the gallery that formed a protective square round the monastery church. In the room was a table, a bed, an icon of the Lord, and a gas lamp that hung from the ceiling by three chains. The walls were covered in a wash of sky blue. Georgiou had been sitting on the bed for just a few moments when the old man who had opened the monastery gate to him appeared with a glass of ouzo and a saucer of Turkish delight, which the locals called *loukoumia*.

"Father Monas bids you welcome," said the old man, placing the offering on the table.

"Thank you," answered Georgiou. "Who is Father Monas?"

"The abbot of the monastery. You are his guest and the guest of the Lord."

Georgiou mumbled his thanks and watched the old man trudge away. He wondered what could have prompted a man to spend his life on this forlorn tower of rock in the middle of nowhere. Though he was Orthodox, Georgiou had never felt confined to the beliefs and practices of the traditional church.

That evening, he stood in the church for an hour and listened to the monks intoning their beautiful chants, *Kyrie Eleison, Kyrie Eleison.* He noticed the tall, thin figure of the abbot, Father Monas, in his black habit that reached to the floor. The father's eyes were closed, though his face seemed full of attention, responding with a quiver, a smile, or a raising of the head to every shift in the music and to each of the silences.

Georgiou, too, was moved, though not as much as the abbot. The fragrance of myrrh reminded him of his childhood, when he had gone often with his father to the small Orthodox church in Florence. The icons at the entrance to the Holy of Holies, he noticed, were several centuries old, in the primitive style of Macedonia, the northern region of Greece where his father had once lived with his mother. One icon in particular caught his attention. It was a Madonna and Child. The Virgin's eyes were filled with a tender sadness, and her face, inclined to embrace the Christ child, was the color of brown olives. In contemplating this Virgin, Georgiou felt her sorrow, live and moist, watering his soul.

9

THE YOUNG MAN was making ready to leave early the next morning when he came across Father Monas by the gatehouse. The abbot's bearing had a simple dignity. Unusually for a Greek, he had blue eyes. Greeting his guest, the abbot asked him where he was going.

Georgiou hesitated, then spoke.

"I am going to Konya. As a pilgrim," he added boldly, remembering Andros's advice to tell the truth. "There was a great saint and poet called Rumi who once lived there. One of his poems moved me so much I had to go."

"A Muslim saint?" the abbot asked.

"Well, yes," Georgiou answered, a little sheepishly. "He was Muslim, but for me he was above all a poet. His words speak to people of all faiths. He touched me in a way I have hardly known before."

"Yes," Father Monas smiled. "And could it be the touch of love that your poet gave you?"

Georgiou reddened a little, and nodded.

"Love," the abbot continued, "is what has kept me here on this mountain for forty-two years."

Father Monas looked at the young man.

"Can you describe this love you are seeking?" he asked.

"I know it when I feel it," Georgiou murmured. "It is a love in which nothing is left out."

"Yes," Father Monas nodded. "And that kind of love is the greatest work a man can do. Yet for everyone it is a different journey. For me, love flowered in this one spot, and I have had no need to go anywhere else. Others need to go far and wide in search of it. It all depends on the seed of your life, which will bear fruit in its own good time. Yet in the end, whatever your destiny has in store, it is always love that finds you, and not the other way around. That is why we must learn to listen."

Georgiou was puzzled by the abbot's words, but he stilled the question on the tip of his tongue and waited. Father Monas fingered for a moment the silver Greek cross that hung from his neck on a thin leather cord. He seemed pensive.

"In our tradition, the most important lesson we have to learn is obedience to God. Most people think this means to be like children who do what the schoolteacher tells them. They do not know that the word *obey* in our Greek language means 'to listen.' To obey God is to listen out for Him in every situation. This is my advice to you, Georgiou. Profit from your time alone, go into yourself, and listen out for the voice that comes unbidden. Listen to that part of you that knows all along what you have to do. This is the intelligence of love; the voice that speaks without complicated explanations, simple and to the point. When you hear that voice, do its bidding. Do not think twice and do not look back."

Georgiou looked at the elderly monk who now held open the thick wooden gate of the monastery for him to leave. Suddenly, he felt grateful to this man who a moment ago had been a stranger.

"That is the voice that told me to go to Konya," Georgiou said, as he stood in the doorway.

"I know." The old monk smiled. "And you will discover that it never stops speaking to you. Only our capacity to listen determines how much we hear it." He paused, tipping his head to one side, as if someone had just whispered in his ear.

"Delphi is not far out of your way to the Holy Mountain, Georgiou. It might be wise of you to stop there and listen for a while. In ancient Greece, even wise men like Socrates would go to the oracle at Delphi. Delphi was a hearing aid, so to speak. You never know how that voice may get through to you.

"And after all," Father Monas continued, "for one who spends his time painting icons of the Blessed Mother, it would only be courtesy to pay your respects to a shrine that was once the sanctuary of Gaia, the Blessed Mother of the Earth. She presided there for centuries, protected by her son, the snake god."

"How did you know I was going to the Holy Mountain?" Georgiou asked, surprised. "There are more direct ways to Turkey than that."

"I try to listen," Father Monas smiled, "and that is what I heard. May God speed you on your way, Georgiou." And shaking the young man's hand, the wise abbot watched Georgiou as he went down the long flight of stone stairs that led to the road through the valley below.

Georgiou paused for a moment at the bottom of the steps. Then he promptly turned south and began to make his way through the lonely valleys of northern Greece, with Mount Parnassus and the sacred shrine of Delphi before him.

10

IT TOOK Georgiou almost six days to walk across the mountains to Delphi, but walking was the way he most loved to travel. It eased him into a rhythm his body and mind were thankful for. It aligned him with the motion of animals, with the occasional goat or mule that passed him on his way. It allowed for conversation with strangers, for a shared pot of sweet tea with the mountain herders. Above all, walking let him feel the ground beneath his feet and the sky over his head. *What else could a human being want?* he would say to himself, as he strode through the steep valleys and over the mountain passes, the birds calling to one another on every side, a rushing river below him, the pines whispering in the wind.

On the sixth day Mount Parnassus was large on the horizon before him, and Delphi was just a few hours away on the lowest slopes. Away to the south, the waters of the Gulf of Corinth glistened blue and white in the afternoon sun. As he walked, Georgiou thought of that traveler of all travelers, Odysseus the ancient Greek; how he must have seen what Georgiou could see before him now. For Ithaca, that adventurer's island home, lay just a few miles away at the mouth of the gulf.

11

GEORGIOU walked into the shrine of Delphi an hour before sunset. Only the guardian was there now, for the tourist season was over, and the ruins were eerily quiet. Three pillars of the original temple were still standing, and the guardian let Georgiou sleep at their base. As night took over from day, Georgiou lay down and gazed up at Sirius, shining like a jewel in the canopy above. He thought of the countless people who had traveled from all around the Aegean Sea to reach this spot in the hope of an answer to their questions. Georgiou, who was normally so full of questions, had none now. It was enough to be here with the stars, and an old Greek pillar at his back.

He was on the verge of sleep when he became aware of something in the grass beside him. Turning, he saw a snake, perhaps five feet long, head raised and forked tongue quivering. The snake stared into him with unblinking eyes before slithering away between the pillars of the temple. Georgiou sat motionless in the dark, every cell awake with attention. For an hour he sat there, but the snake did not return. He remembered what Father Monas had said about the temple, how it was originally dedicated to the Blessed Mother of the Earth and protected by her son, the snake god.

Father Monas said I should listen, thought Georgiou. *Perhaps this is the kind of listening he means.*

Georgiou slept deeply that night, but early in the morning he awoke with a start. He had been dreaming one of those dreams that is more like a vision, the kind that has an uncommon light and sharpness of image. He saw—as real as any human form in the light of day—a single image of Our Lady, in the form he had painted so often, except that her face was dark. Her head was inclined to the left, and a tear was falling from her eye. Along with the image he heard a voice—as real as any he might hear in a normal conversation—that said:

> *I am not the One you are looking for. I am not the One, yet that One is no different to me.*

Georgiou was filled with—how could this be possible?—both joy and sorrow at the same time. For the whole of the next day, he sat quietly, stirred by deep feelings.

A couple of tourists from Athens came and went. Georgiou stayed quietly by his pillar, still full with the presence of his dream. He pondered the Dark Mary's words and wondered who he might be looking for; he hadn't been aware he was looking for anyone. He was going to Konya because he was impelled to do so, without any expectation of the outcome. He remembered the counsel of his friend Andros, to pay heed to his dreams, and he took care not to let his Greek rationality get the better of him.

It means what it means, and I am thankful to have been visited by such a grace, Georgiou said to himself. He remembered, too, that Father Monas had told him that the ancient oracle of Delphi had always spoken in riddles and paradox, and here was a riddle if ever he had heard one.

Before the day was out, Georgiou had unpacked his artist's materials and had begun a sketch of the vision the oracle had given him. He would paint an icon in honor of the Dark Mother.

12

THE GUARDIAN of the oracle at Delphi was an old man whose family lived in the village below. For the first few days after Georgiou's arrival, he would stop now and then to watch him at work on his icon. One day he appeared with the village priest.

"Sir," the priest said, "I have a kind favor to ask you. Our villagers have a deep veneration for a holy icon of the Blessed Virgin, one that has been in our church for generations. It has received so many kisses that it is worn down to the wood. I have had to replace it with another, far less favored by my flock. Since the original icon was put away, the fortunes of the village have declined. It would be an honor if you could restore it for us."

"I do not think I will be here long enough to restore your icon," Georgiou told the guardian and the priest. "I have a long journey to make, to Turkey, and the days will be getting shorter soon."

The priest was visibly saddened, for restorers of icons rarely passed through the mountain villages, and the appearance of the young man had seemed like a grace from the Virgin Mary herself. The parish would never have enough money to hire an artist to travel out from Athens.

Georgiou felt the man's sadness. He realized that he, too, was feeling a certain disappointment with himself. *Why can I not offer a few days of my time to a village that has asked for it?* he thought. *Is my time so precious that I cannot respond to another's need? This is a blessed place, and it has already given me a gift that I shall never forget. I am ashamed of my meanness.*

He looked up at the priest and said, "Father, I have changed my mind. I shall restore your icon. I will come to the church tomorrow, though I shall return to the temple in the evenings. It suits me well here."

The priest, delighted, went off to share the news with the village folk, for it was a Sunday and many of them would be in the church that evening.

The next morning Georgiou laid aside the icon that he had begun painting after the vision of the Mother and went down to the village. The villagers' icon was in a delicate state, and all of Georgiou's attention and skill were needed to bring it back to life again. The days soon turned into weeks. The Gulf of Corinth turned gray as often as it was blue.

Each evening, when he returned to the ancient pillars, he would find a parcel of food from one or another of the villagers, and always a sprig of basil and some olives. Sometimes, when the wind blew colder than usual, he would spend the evening with the temple guardian in his little hut. The guardian's name was Kriti—at least, that is what everyone called him, because he originally came from Crete. Kriti would often share his meal with Georgiou, though he rarely spoke more than a few words at a time.

He is only a simple villager, Georgiou mused to himself one evening, as they sat there in silence. *But even he has a gruff kindness to share.*

13

One evening, just before Georgiou finished his work of restoration, Kriti began to tell him a strange thing.

"I have lived under the protection of this oracle for seven years now," he said, handing Georgiou some thick dark bread. "The government pays me a little to guard the site, but in truth it is I who am protected. The Dark Mother came to me once in a dream, soon after I started here, and told me things no man should ever know. I am Orthodox now, as ever, but I tell you on my life that the ancient people who built this place knew the Holy Mother as surely as we do. They only called Her by a different name."

The young man started. He had never told a soul about the vision he had had on his first night at the shrine.

"What do you mean, Kriti, the Dark Mother?" he asked.

"I think you know what I mean, Georgiou," Kriti replied, glancing at him briefly and then returning his gaze to the fire. "Whenever I look at you I see the snake at your feet. She has come to you, too. I know it."

"It is true," Georgiou murmured. "I had a vision of the Sacred Mother on my first night here. I knew Her instantly, except her face was blacker than the oldest icon. Why is that so, Kriti? Why does Our Lady appear in this place as dark?"

"Our Lady is dark here because her wisdom is of the night. In the oldest of our icons you will know that her cloak is sown with a thousand stars. She is the womb from which all things emerge and have their being. She is wild and dark because She is Life itself. Like life, She summons our demons as well as our angels."

"Then why is the Holy Mother so gentle and merciful in our tradition?" the young man asked. "I always thought that She was the heart of compassion."

"She is that indeed," the older man replied. "But the ancients who built this place knew that the source of all compassion is Truth. And the Truth is beyond any ideas of right and wrong."

The light of the fire flickered across Kriti's face. Shadows danced behind him on the hut wall. He and Georgiou had barely exchanged more than the usual pleasantries in the preceding weeks, and the younger man felt humbled by the knowledge of this unassuming old man.

"Please tell me, then, Kriti," he asked. "If the Holy Mother is not gentle and merciful, what is She?"

Kriti smiled.

"She *is* that. She is Our Lady of Great Compassion because She embraces all of us without ceasing, without judgment, whoever we are. But She is also mighty. She is terrible, wrathful even, when She wants to shake us free from the grip of our illusions."

The two men sat together in silence, the greener wood crackling on the fire.

"Kriti," Georgiou said at length, "Our Lady said something to me when She came to me. She said that She was not the one I was looking for, but the one I was seeking was no different to her. Could you tell me what She meant? It seems like a riddle to me."

Kriti laughed a long, low laugh.

"It is a riddle indeed," he replied. "And one that you alone will solve."

Georgiou fell silent. *This journey is like no other,* he thought, as he got up to go to his bed at the foot of the pillar.

"What do you expect from a journey of love?" chuckled the old guardian, as if Georgiou had spoken aloud. "Anything becomes possible. You draw down forces that you can only bow to."

A week later, Georgiou's work on the village icon was finally finished. While the whole village turned out for a grand procession down the main street and around the church in honor of the newly restored icon, Georgiou made ready to be on his way. He was bound for the Holy Mountain of Athos.

As he was leaving, Kriti came to shake his hand.

"Young man," he said, "you have been blessed to make these people happy. Know, then, that kindness is the first and last step on the road of love; and yet the first step and the last are not the same. Kindness, as we know from our Blessed Mother, is fierce and mighty as well gentle and forgiving. Either one can open a door in your heart and change both you and the world."

Georgiou thanked the old guardian for his words. They embraced, and then Kriti watched the painter disappear over the rise of the hill.

14

ATHOS—the entire peninsula—is a country within the country of Greece. It answers only to the Patriarch of Constantinople, whose residence is in Istanbul, and who is the head of the Orthodox Church. The Holy Mountain lies at the far end of this finger of land, some twenty miles long, that juts out into the northern Aegean. No woman has set foot anywhere on that skinny peninsula for almost two thousand years. The monks say that the Virgin Mary was shipwrecked on the shores of Athos after the Crucifixion, and as she stepped ashore she claimed the land for her own. That is why, they say, no other woman can go there. Only monks live on Athos, and their monasteries are spread out all over the wild and wooded peninsula, with nothing more than footpaths to connect them.

The monks of Athos—Greeks, Russians, Serbs, Romanians, Bulgarians—have ordered their lives by the Byzantine calendar, some five hours behind the rest of Greece. They have set themselves adrift from the rest of the world. Great mystics and miracle workers have lived there down through the centuries, inspiring many to follow them. A steady stream of novices, tired or disillusioned with modern life, has kept these ancient communities alive.

Georgiou staggered ashore from the little boat onto the dock of the tiny port. The boat, the only means of access to Athos, was laden with pilgrims. It had plied its way for two hours along the peninsula, dipping and rolling in the heavy swell. Now all Georgiou wanted was to lay his head on solid ground. But it was a three-hour walk to the monastery of Iveron, and it was already afternoon.

Georgiou set off along a worn, narrow path, up into the hills. Trees crowded in on the little track, and the only sound came from birds, hundreds of them, it seemed, on every side. Now and then through the trees he caught a glimpse of the glistening ocean, far below him already. Sometimes, the path petered out in the forest of twisted and stunted pines, and he would stumble this way and that before finding it again. Sometimes he heard the call of an animal, and wondered if there were wolves on Athos still. With every step he felt lighter, fed by the southern light, the air, the sharp cut of tree against deep blue sky.

It was in this buoyant mood, his lungs full of the scent of juniper and thyme, that Georgiou came in sight, finally, of the great monastery of Iveron. At the gate, an old monk lay sleeping, his shoes by his side. Georgiou hesitated for an instant, then stepped on through the gateway to find himself in a large courtyard with a church in the middle.

15

FATHER DIMITRI sat alone in his painter's studio, a small hut in the monastery grounds, on the edge of the cliff. For thirty years he had gazed upon this same stretch of ocean, ever since he had left his hometown of Thessaloníki to take up the monastic life. He and his brother Andros had shared a fierce love of life's mysteries, but their stories had diverged when they were still young men. Whereas Dimitri was solitary by nature, given to inner contemplation of the Christian mysteries, Andros was more questioning, less bound to tradition.

Yet, for all the differences in their lifestyles and paths, Dimitri and Andros were closer now in their later years than ever. They wrote long letters describing their various realizations and disillusions, and came to see that their lives were not so different after all. Dimitri had followed the Orthodox teachings down into their silent source, and Andros had for years known the stillness where all religions meet. Freedom, they both understood now, could only mean freedom from their own preconceptions.

Once, in a crisis of faith, Andros had written to his brother and asked if he, too, should enter the monastic life. Dimitri had drawn a picture of the Buddha and sent it to Andros, who immediately understood. He should stand by his own story: like the Buddha, he was destined to find his own way, and that was a path every bit as honorable and formidable as one that confines a man to a cell for thirty years.

Dimitri picked up a paintbrush and dipped it into the dark brown pigment in the pot in front of his sketch. With slow, downward strokes, he started to paint the face of the Virgin. This icon, he knew it, would be different from anything he had done before. He was finally ready, after all this time, to bring into the world the face that had been burned on his inner eye all those years ago.

Then into his thoughts came a knock on the door.

16

FATHER DIMITRI unlatched the door and opened it wide. Georgiou stood there, breathing heavily in the warm sea breeze, his letter of introduction in his hand. Dimitri welcomed his guest inside.

"My brother speaks highly of you," he smiled, putting the open letter down on the table. "Please allow me to finish this coat of paint before it dries. I need only a moment more."

It surprised Georgiou to see the icon the monk was working on. His eyes took in the single row of books on a wooden shelf, the iron bed, the small crucifix on the wall.

"Andros says in his letter that you are on an interesting journey," Dimitri said when they had both sat down. "I would like to hear what you have come across along the way."

Georgiou told him about his stay in Delphi and his vision of the Dark Mother. Taking the sketch from his bag, he explained how he had started to paint what he had seen.

"Then you have come to a fitting place," Dimitri said. "We can work here together, if you wish, since we are both, as you have seen, absorbed in the same icon."

"Tell me, Father," Georgiou replied, "what is it that led you to paint this icon? Its vision of womanhood seems to be quite different from the teachings of the church."

Father Dimitri sat back in his chair and was silent for a moment.

"When I first came to Athos, I was told that the only safe way even to think of a woman was as my mother. In all other guises, I was told, they are a distraction from the path of inner contemplation. We have taken up this life to direct our attention beyond the world of the senses, toward the invisible ground. That is our way, though I know now that fear also plays a part in it. I know, too, that there are other ways. Our brothers in Islam, the dervishes, have never favored removing themselves from the world, yet there is no doubt that they have produced as many great saints as our blessed church."

"So do you still think of all women as your mother?" the young man asked.

Father Dimitri's soft, dark eyes glanced over at Georgiou.

"You see the great ocean out there," he said, looking out his painter's window. "However many waves of different height and color there are, they are all the many faces of the one ocean. I have not seen a woman now for thirty years, so womanhood is for me like that endless stretch of water, all embracing, all nourishing, beautiful to behold. Just like the icons of our Blessed Mother. Yet in my time here, the many different faces of woman have arisen in my mind like the waves, and I have come to understand that they are all noble expressions of the one Original Beauty. So to answer your question, Georgiou, I have come to honor woman in all her guises. And because of this, I have come, too, to honor my own body, its earthly longings and desires."

Father Dimitri's words took Georgiou by surprise.

"You mean, after all these years, you still have longings and desires of the flesh?"

Dimitri smiled.

"I still have a body," he said quietly. "Mercifully, I am no longer afraid of its longings and the images they cast into my mind. These days, I am glad to belong to the earth and the life of the senses. Heaven is nowhere if not here. Would you agree?"

Georgiou had never before met a monk who spoke so freely as this.

"I would agree," he replied finally. "But how is it these things are no longer a distraction from your contemplations?"

"Because I know now that the silent source is everywhere, in everything that lives and breathes. It does not pick and choose, saying I take this flower for my own, but this cockroach I disown. The true Mother embraces all, including our longings and desires. If we see Her in everything, everything will lead us to Her. That is what has led me to paint this icon you see here now."

Georgiou stood up and bent over Dimitri's painting.

"She reminds me of the Song of Solomon," he murmured.

I am black and comely,
Dark as the tents of Kedar . . .

"That is a compliment I am glad to hear," murmured Father Dimitri. "This Blessed Virgin is indeed comely. She is the ocean, mighty and terrible, beautiful and calm. She refuses nothing. She celebrates both worlds, time and eternity. I pray that I have the vision and the courage to show Her in her true colors."

The two painters, the young and the not so young, sat well into the evening discussing their art. The gas lights in the monastery went out one by one, the last prayers were sung. Georgiou slept that night on the icon painter's floor, to be awakened at daybreak by the smell of thick Greek coffee simmering on the old black stove.

17

GEORGIOU accepted Father Dimitri's invitation to stay at his studio and finish his icon of the Blessed Dark Mother. Each morning the two of them worked with their brushes, mostly in silence. Every evening Georgiou went to the monastery church to listen to the fine singing of the monks, and in the early afternoons he would spend an hour or two in the monastery library. The libraries on Athos still held some of the most ancient and precious books in Europe. The oldest copy of the Gospel of John, written down in Greek in the fourth century, was in a glass case in the library of the Grand Lavra, the largest monastery on the peninsula.

Iveron had its share of treasures, too. Georgiou found books there, all of them with thick leather bindings engraved with the cross, that led him into the world of the early Christians who went to live in the desert; to the Arab knowledge of geometry and mathematics, to the principles of sacred architecture, to medieval anatomy.

From all his readings, one line of the desert fathers intrigued him more than anything else. "Watch and pray. Above all things, be vigilant," it said.

"What did the desert fathers mean, Dimitri," he asked one day as they were taking their coffee, "when they spoke of being vigilant?"

"They were referring to the way the mind is susceptible to invisible influences," Dimitri replied enigmatically.

"Now you are speaking in riddles more elusive than theirs," smiled Georgiou.

"Without even knowing it, the mind jumps on the back of each passing wave," Dimitri went on. "But if you pay attention, you will become aware of something that doesn't move, however good or bad things seem. Your poet, Rumi the dervish, knew this well. He spoke of this 'something' as being like a field we can lie down in."

Out beyond all wrongdoing and rightdoing,
There is a field. I'll meet you there.
When the soul lies down in that grass,
The world is too full to speak about . . .

"How is it that you know the poetry of Rumi?" Georgiou asked. "He is a Muslim, and you are Orthodox."

Father Dimitri glanced gently at his companion. "We monks are not all as rigid in our beliefs as you may imagine," he smiled. "Our dervish brothers have come to Athos for many hundreds of years, and we in our turn have had dialogue with them in Constantinople since the fall of that city to the Turks. It is said that the dervishes are the ones who first taught our forefathers on Athos the prayer of the heart. Only the words were changed."

"What is the prayer of the heart?" asked Georgiou.

"It is the vigilance the desert fathers were speaking about," Dimitri replied. "They are one and the same. Whatever you feel or do, wherever you are, you let your breath carry the mind down into the heart. When the mind is joined to the heart, the quality of presence arises. Being aware of the passage of breath down into the chest helps you become present. You remember that it is not you who breathes; it is the breath that breathes you. And you feel gratitude for that breathing presence.

"What a miracle it is," Dimitri went on. "Whenever you look for it, the breath is there, breathing you full of life's electricity. What compassion life has for us all. Some like to murmur a word or a phrase as they breathe out, such as the name of Jesus; for the dervishes, it is Allah. Others prefer simply to feel the aaah! flow in and out, filling them with being. It is not the words that make a prayer, it is the devotion. Then, whatever happens, whether we feel exalted or laid low, it all happens within the embrace of the breath. That is what it means to watch and pray. Simple, but it means a lifetime of renunciation."

Georgiou was puzzled.

"Why do you say a renunciation?" he asked. "I don't see why you need to wear a monk's habit, or be celibate, to follow your breath down into the heart."

"That is true," Dimitri replied. "These are external things. I have come to see, in my years on this mountain, that the true renunciation concerns our attention. If you are going to be aware of your breath in this way, in whatever you do, it requires a shifting of your attention from life's highs and lows to the silent source. Not that the waves stop rising and falling—they always will—but that you are aware of the deep current beneath them all. Tomorrow, if you wish, I shall take you to meet someone who has lived in those depths for a lifetime."

The rest of that day the two men were silent, absorbed in their icons.

18

THE NEXT morning, Father Dimitri led Georgiou out along the cliffs by way of a dusty, winding path. After they had walked for an hour or more, Dimitri pointed ahead to a tiny hut perched below the cliff over the gleaming ocean.

"That is the home of Father Sofroniou," Dimitri said. "He is a hermit and, some say, a saint. Every week, a boat sails by, and he hauls up his supplies from it in a wicker basket. There are many solitaries who live like this on Athos. They never leave their huts for anything, not even Communion."

"I thought you had to have communion to be Orthodox," Georgiou said.

"When you are in communion, you have no need of Communion," Dimitri replied.

As they clambered down the steep path toward the hut, a stooping, disheveled old man in rags appeared in the doorway. He did not seem to fit Georgiou's idea of a saint. Even though they were still a hundred yards away, Georgiou could see that the old man was scowling at them. As they drew closer, he reached into a bucket by the door and began raining his visitors with stones.

Georgiou stopped in his tracks, cowering, his arms over his head to protect himself. The cliff was steep, the path narrow; they could easily have fallen into the ocean attempting to avoid the old man's assault. He was about to turn back, when Dimitri walked on by him without any attempt to shield himself from the stones.

"Keep going," Dimitri said, as he passed by. "Watch your breath. Do not lose your attention to your judgments or your fear."

Georgiou did as he was told, but it was all he could do to stay on the path. The stones seemed aimed at him rather than Dimitri, and when one of them hit him on the leg he cried out in anger.

"Breathe," Dimitri called over his shoulder. "Pay no attention to your thoughts."

Sofroniou continued to throw stones until the pair had finally reached his door. Then the old man turned and went inside without a word. Georgiou, flustered and confused, followed Father Dimitri in. The room was bare except for a table, a chair, and an icon of Christ. Georgiou watched as Dimitri went up to Sofroniou and kissed him on both cheeks, and then motioned to Georgiou to do the same. As Georgiou stepped forward to embrace the old man, his nose was filled with the old man's stink. He cringed.

"Who is this smelly creature you bring to me?" the old man asked, with a fiery glance at Dimitri.

"He is a traveler from Italy, a painter of icons, holy father," Dimitri replied.

The old man scoffed.

"This man is no painter. He is a fool. That is why I stoned you," he continued, turning to Georgiou. "To wake you up from your foolishness. But no doubt I was wasting my time. I see you are full of romance. The romance of the longing, the wandering. Yet in all your questing, have you ever stopped to wonder, Who is it that is longing?"

"I don't know," Georgiou mumbled, thoroughly disoriented and confused.

"Then there is hope," Sofroniou answered, as gruff as ever, stroking his matted beard. "Not knowing, that is the secret cup. Not knowing does not mean giving up on the question, young man. It means not settling for an easy answer. Live the question. Feel it in your core. Who are you in truth? This question is the great work. But to answer it, you must be willing to cut off your head and sit on it."

Georgiou was stunned by Sofroniou's words. Who would want to cut off their head and sit on it?

"Go deeper than the words themselves," Sofroniou said. "Remember, do not settle for answers. Find out who is asking the question. Only then will you greet yourself arriving at your own door."

Georgiou thought it best not to respond. They sat there for a few minutes in silence. Then Father Dimitri rose from the dirt floor and embraced Sofroniou once more. Georgiou followed suit. This time, he noticed a sweetness in the air.

They started back along the path, the water below them glistening in the sun, a lone buzzard turning and wheeling above the cliffs. As they walked, Georgiou was suddenly aware that his head was empty of thoughts, and that he felt unusually content.

19

FOR MANY days Georgiou worked alongside Father Dimitri, laboring to give expression to the deep tenderness that he knew his icon was calling for. But the Dark Mother was proving elusive, and Dimitri suggested that he might serve the work better by walking the paths of the Athos peninsula for a while.

So Georgiou began to wander the byways of the Holy Mountain and visit some of the other monasteries there. He would walk for hours at a time through the low, dense forests of oak and pine, often without passing another human being. The sun was usually low on the horizon when he arrived at the gates of a monastery, and he was glad for the customary welcome of a glass of ouzo and a small tray of *loukoumia*.

Georgiou met many refugees from the ways of the world on his wanderings from monastery to monastery. In the Serbian house, he found two old men who had once worked together in a chocolate factory outside Paris. They were refugees from the troubles in the Balkans sharing a small rented room in the Bastille area. One evening, after work, one of them picked up the Serbian newspaper and read a plea from the Serbian Monastery on Athos for novices. If there were no new blood soon, the article said, the monastery would have to close its doors on a history of five hundred years. The two friends looked at each other, and there and then decided to go. Now they were the only monks left in the monastery. They had not seen the world beyond Athos since, and were as content as ever with their simple life on the Holy Mountain.

How blessed some people are, thought Georgiou, as he left the Serbian house and went on his way, *to have found their life's calling so gracefully.* Yet he knew that he, too, was blessed in his own way. *Blessings must be present in everyone's life,* he thought to himself. *If only we can see through their disguises.*

In the Greek house of Stavronikita, another, much younger man told Georgiou how he had been reared in a Greek family in London and had become the assistant to a famous fashion designer there. He had lived London's social life to the full, all the while feeling himself become more and more empty. He began to return to the religion of his childhood, and eventually, the pull to come to Athos as a monk proved irresistible.

This same young man led Georgiou to the ossuary, the vault where the bones of the departed were stacked: skulls all in rows, with thighbones heaped up below them. Two of the skulls were golden in color, and the monk told Georgiou that these were the skulls of saints; for only those whose skulls became gold were later pronounced to be holy ones. He had come to Athos, the young man said, that he might die with a golden skull. "If it be the Lord's will," he added.

I am glad for him, that he is so sure of what he wants, Georgiou thought as he went on his way. *As for me, I have no wish to be a saint. My wish is to belong fully in this world, rather than to set my sights on the next.*

In the Grand Lavra, the most ancient monastery of all, Georgiou met a young man in the throes of doubt and despair. Fired with the vision of finding a great master, he had left his life in Athens and spent three years as a disciple of one of the hermits who lived on the Holy Mountain. The old man had made him build walls all day long and then tear them down again the next day. He would not let him read anything except the Bible, or sleep anywhere but on the floor.

The young man had to defer to the hermit in every detail of his waking day and had to serve him as occasion demanded. Instead of breaking him free of his self-will, this treatment served only to send the boy into a deep and dark depression. Finally, unable to perceive any wise motive for the hermit's odd methods, he sought refuge in the Grand Lavra—only to discover there that his experience was a common one among the fresh young men eager for the holy life who turned up every year on the mountain.

The young man's story reminded Georgiou of his strange reception by Sofroniou. Yet Georgiou knew that his encounter with the old man had added a richness to his life. *There is no formula for this journey,* he thought. *Every life seems to have its own intelligent course.*

Once, on the path between the Grand Lavra and Pantaleimon Monastery, Georgiou came across a man in rags standing on one leg under a tree, his hands and face lifted to heaven. At his feet were offerings of food and water. Two other monks were kneeling before him. As they got up to go, Georgiou asked them what the man was doing.

"He is offering penance," one of the monks told the young man from Florence. "He has been in that same position without moving for five years. He has not eaten in all that time, though some people still leave food offerings before him."

"How long will he stay there?" Georgiou asked.

"Until the Lord lifts his spirit to heaven," the other monk said.

"But why? Why does he need to torture himself so?"

"It is not torture for him," the first monk replied. "He is joyful at having vanquished the demands of the flesh."

Georgiou felt sad, even so, at the sight of the man on one leg. He walked on a little, and suddenly, there between a cleft in the hills, the sky became one with the sea in a haze of gold and blue. Georgiou stood for a long moment gazing in wonder. It was as if the world had called to him suddenly, reminding him that all was well with it, and to call it by its true name, which was Beauty.

20

GEORGIOU returned to Father Dimitri's studio and continued painting. The days turned into weeks, the melodic orations of the monks in the church began to seep into Georgiou's bones, the light on the ocean delighted his eyes, the quiet attention of the older painter slowly steadied his mind. His icon of the Blessed Dark Mother began to take firm and delicate shape. She was an unusual Virgin, her long dark hair gathered in a silver clasp. At last, he came to the finishing touch, the tear in the corner of her eye. On that day, Georgiou wondered out loud whether Athos might not be a fine place to live out a life after all.

"It is the past that lives on here," Dimitri smiled when Georgiou voiced his thoughts. "You are a child of the future, and your life will take you on from the Holy Mountain and over the straits to the great city of Istanbul. Let what you have found here remain with you in spirit, and it will serve you well. Here, we live in eternity, while the rest of the world lives in time.

You must learn to live in both, and that is why you must go on your way."

The next morning Georgiou awoke, took some coffee from the stove, and wandered over to his easel to look at his work. He bent in astonishment over his painting. There, where he had painted the tear of the Virgin the day before, was a bead of water. Below it, a moist rivulet ran down to the foot of the icon, without seeming to have harmed or loosened the paint. He motioned to Father Dimitri. The older man gazed at the drop of water, then turned to the young man and held out his hand.

"Your work is done here," said Dimitri. "The Dark Mother has received you. It is time for you to continue on the road to Konya, which some call the road of love. The only protection you will need is vigilance, the kind that joins your mind to your heart. For the rest, you are blessed indeed, for She will be with you, even in the darkest hour. Remember, Georgiou, watch, and pray the prayer that has no words."

Georgiou knew that he was blessed indeed. The following morning, he took his leave of Father Dimitri and continued on the road to Konya. Dimitri waited until the young man had turned the bend in the path, and went back to take up his brushes.

21

GEORGIOU went down to Dafni, the port of the Holy Mountain, and boarded the boat to the mainland. Back through the choppy waters they plied, and Georgiou was pale and shaky when they finally came into harbor. As he stepped ashore, a couple of young women passed along the dock, laughing and throwing their heads of long hair back in the wind. They were the first women Georgiou had seen in months, yet they seemed the most ordinary sight in the world. *Ordinary and beautiful,* thought Georgiou, watching them disappear into the crowd.

The young icon painter took the road east to the border with Turkey, his Blessed Dark Mother safe in the satchel on his back. As he went, Georgiou sang softly beneath his breath. Old melodies without words welled up from his childhood, songs of praise and lament he had barely given a thought to in years. His step was light; there was peace in his heart.

22

GEORGIOU crossed the border into Turkey. It was the first time he had ever set foot on the land of the ancient enemies of his Greek ancestors. The road to Istanbul led first to Edirne, and Georgiou reached that city just before nightfall. Men sat huddled outside the cafés, their hookah pipes bubbling in unison. People milled in the narrow lanes of the bazaar (the Turks called it the *soukh*). The smell of spices mingled with wood smoke. At the door of an inn a beggar lay, his hand outstretched, his eyes beseeching. Georgiou gave him some alms and pushed the door open.

There were only men inside, two of them in the traditional robe, the *jelabeh,* of the Arab. One or two wore the wide blue pantaloons of old Turkey, while the rest were dressed in Western style. Georgiou took the last room. He had barely closed the door and sat on the bed when a cry went up from somewhere outside. It was the muezzin, the man who calls the faithful to prayer. It was the most haunting call that Georgiou had ever heard. As the cry rang into the night, *Allah hu Akbar, Allah hu Akbar,* it struck his heart and tears welled instantly down his cheeks. *Allah hu Akbar,* he found himself murmuring, although he had never spoken a word of the Arab language before. God is great, God is great. In every tongue and land the people praise him. And the last words on Georgiou's tongue that night, as he fell into sleep, were those. *Allah hu Akbar, Allah hu Akbar.*

23

WHEN GEORGIOU stepped out of the inn the next morning, the beggar he had given alms to was waiting by the door.

"Sir, you were generous to me last night," said the man as Georgiou made to pass him. "I want to repay you in my own fashion. It would be my honor to show you the music sanatorium."

Georgiou had never heard of a music sanatorium, and thought the old beggar might be mad. But then he remembered the message about kindness from the guardian at Delphi. So, not knowing where he was being led, Georgiou followed the man through the streets of the town. They wound their way through the *soukh* and out the other side to a slight rise where the buildings began to give way to patches of green. There before them stood a large building with several wings, surrounded by gardens that had fallen into neglect.

The beggar hurried toward an octagonal pavilion in the center of the building. He pushed open the old wooden door and ushered Georgiou into a large white room that was empty of all furnishings. Above them was a dome painted all the way round with a serpent with scales that was almost biting its tail. The floor, like the walls, was made of pale stone slabs. A stone bench followed the wall round each of its eight sides. The man motioned to Georgiou to sit with him.

Within moments, several other people had entered and taken seats on the bench alongside them. Some appeared to be as poor as the beggar. A few seemed troubled and were led to their places by friends. Gradually, the stone bench filled up with men and women from every class of society. Finally, two men in white robes came in and sat on the floor in the middle of the room, beneath the dome.

The men wore round white hats and had long gray beards. One of them had an oud, the Turkish lute, and the other had a *ney,* the wooden flute favored by the dervishes in their ceremonies. They sat quietly for a moment; then, after murmuring a prayer, they began to play. The sound rose to the dome, spread out over the walls, and filled the whole octagon with beauty. Something deep stirred in Georgiou's heart. The beggar by his side swayed gently backward and forward, his eyes closed, a beatific smile on his face. Those who were troubled were stilled, those who were sad were reassured, the creased faces of the careworn were softened.

For a time beyond time the musicians played. When they finally put their instruments down and padded softly out of the building, Georgiou no longer knew how long he had been there. Every cell in his body was humming with the music. He felt whole, fearful of nothing.

"Who are those men?" he asked the beggar when they were outside again.

"They are dervishes of the Mevlevi Order," said the beggar. "The order of mystics that Rumi founded. In their kindness they have started the ancient music going again. This building was famous all over the Ottoman Empire in years past. It was a sanatorium for the sick of mind, and the cure was music. Over the course of the centuries, the dervishes perfected the art of modulating and healing the emotions with sound. They would use different instruments and minor keys to bring health to the sick of mind, and even of body."

The beggar paused for a moment, and then went on.

"Their devotion was the greater part of their healing power," he said. "They became lost in the divine, and their listeners would forget their ills and be carried away with them. Now these men have chosen to revive the custom, and people are coming here to be healed again."

Without another word, the man bent his head. Then he turned and strode off purposefully toward the town.

24

GEORGIOU continued his journey, traveling for days on the high road to Istanbul, old Constantinople, the great city where the continents of Europe and Asia meet, struggle, and sometimes unite. Long before he reached the outskirts of the city, he could see the minarets of the Blue Mosque, the old Byzantine cathedral Hagia Sophia, soaring like needles over the gray Bosphorus. He could see the steamers snaking their way from shore to shore. He could hear the ships' horns, glimpse some of the great boulevards, and could only imagine what a tumult of humanity awaited him below.

When he reached the first streets, he showed someone the address that his friend Andros had given him and was directed to the great bazaar of the city, the covered *soukh* on the Asian side. The *soukh* in Edirne had done nothing to prepare Georgiou for the Istanbul *soukh* and its vast warren of alleys. Every trade had its own lanes, every lane was packed with stalls and thronged with people. Beggars cried out for alms, women bustled by with children at their skirts, musicians played with a hat at their feet; men sat at little tables playing cards and backgammon, the sweet smell of Turkish coffee was everywhere, the cries of the vendors filled the air.

The exaltation Georgiou had felt in the music sanatorium had stayed with him all the days of travel on the open road to Istanbul. Now, in the *soukh,* it was ebbing away, and he was beginning to feel alone and lost in a foreign world. The address he had been given was of a stall in the *soukh*'s musical instrument section. He was looking for one Hassan Shushud, a master craftsman of the *ney,* Andros had told him. Georgiou wandered up and down the alleys and, after being misdirected several times, finally came upon the area that specialized in musical instruments.

Only one man had heard of Hassan Shushud. He told Georgiou that Hassan had moved his stall out of the *soukh* some time previously and now only sold his work to private customers who came to his house.

"I do not know where Hassan Shushud lives," said the man, whose name was Hakim. "But you are welcome to be my guest if you wish. You have come far, and any man who is a friend of the *ney* is a friend of mine."

Georgiou told him he would be grateful for a bed for the night in this large and unfamiliar city. The two men had tea, and then Hakim led the young Greek through the labyrinth of alleys and out onto a dark backstreet that reeked of the blood of goats. It was the place where sacrifices were made by people who wanted favors from God, Hakim said, his face breaking into a crooked grin. The devout would have a goat killed, then go into the nearby mosque to offer their prayers.

They walked on through cobbled streets until Hakim finally stopped at the door of a dilapidated building and motioned to Georgiou to go inside. At the top of a flight of steps was a room, empty but for a bed with some tattered blankets on it. Hakim said he would be downstairs, and would wake the young man in the morning.

Georgiou sat on the bed and looked about the bare room. For the first time since he had left Florence, he felt lonely. Perhaps he had come far enough, he thought. He had already passed through enough joys and adventures to last him a long time. He thought of his father and his friend Andros, how they must be missing him, as he was them. In a pensive mood, he undressed and put his satchel by the bed. He paused, then picked up the satchel again and tucked it under his head for a pillow. Then he fell into a heavy sleep.

Georgiou awoke with a start at sunrise and noticed that the door to the room was open.

Sunbeams lit up thousands of dust motes dancing. He leaned over to pick up his clothes and saw that his pockets had been turned inside out. His watch, his wallet, and all his money gone. A chill ran down Georgiou's back. He was in a strange city without a penny to his name. He knew no one. He did not even know where he was.

Some reflex made him turn and open his satchel. The Blessed Dark Mother was there, the mark where tears had flowed still visible down her face. He gazed at her and felt a quiet relief.

25

HE PULLED ON his clothes, went down the stairs, and opened the door on the first floor. The room was used to house animals. Inside, a couple of goats were tethered to the wall. Georgiou went out onto the street and followed it downhill, the way they had come the night before. He wandered through the narrow streets until he came to a large boulevard.

There, on the corner, the two Arabs he had seen in the inn at Edirne were talking to a man who was selling birds in gaily colored cages. They smiled in recognition as Georgiou approached and asked him where he was going. Georgiou explained what had happened and said he was looking for a man called Hassan Shushud. The bird seller looked up.

"I know Hassan Shushud," he said quietly. "Who is it that seeks him?"

Georgiou pulled his letter of introduction from his satchel and showed it to the man. The man read it, folded it up, and handed it back to Georgiou.

"Hassan does sell his flutes in the bazaar," he said, "but not in the main music quarter. He is in the old *soukh,* in the music alley there. You strayed into the newer *soukh,* which was built only a hundred years ago and is much larger than the original one. I will send my boy to show you the way. You should go now, because it is Friday and Hassan is sure to be leaving early for the mosque."

Georgiou thanked the man, shook hands with the Arabs, and followed the bird seller's boy into the crowd.

26

GEORGIOU followed his guide through the labyrinth of alleys, almost running to keep up with him. Finally the boy stopped at a stall stacked with flutes and other instruments where two men were drinking tea and laughing together. The boy leaned over to one of the men and whispered in his ear. Hassan Shushud looked up at Georgiou. With a slight bow of greeting, Georgiou reached into his satchel and held out the letter from Andros to Hassan.

"I have not seen Andros in several years," said Hassan, after reading the letter and putting it to one side. "I hold him in the deepest regard. You are welcome here, my friend. From what Andros tells me in his letter, you seem to be chasing Rumi."

Georgiou recounted his journey to the two men and recited the lines that had inspired it. He told them how his money had been stolen the night before, and how he still hoped to reach Konya. Hassan liked the young man. He could see his integrity as if it were a soft light around his body. He could see more than he was ready to say. He invited Georgiou to attend the *sema* that evening, the ceremony of dance and music in which the Mevlevi dervishes offer their devotion to God. He explained that both he and his friend Ali Bey were dervishes of the Mevlevi Order, and that dervishes were also called Sufis.

"What is a Sufi?" Georgiou asked Hassan. The older man paused for a moment.

"A Sufi is a lover of God," he said finally, "one who offers his heart and soul to the One who is beyond all names. The Sufis are the mystics of Islam. We seek the experience of the Beloved. We call to Him to descend into the chamber of our soul. There are many orders of Sufis, or dervishes, as we are also called. Each one was started by the inspiration of a great saint, or sheikh.

"Our order is called the Mevlevi. For a Mevlevi, music and dance are the royal road to union with the Beloved. They fill him with such an ecstasy that sometimes he never returns. Our founding sheikh was called Jelaluddin Rumi. Perhaps that is why Andros sent you to me." He smiled.

"And what is the *sema* that you have invited me to this evening?" asked Georgiou.

"You will see in good time," Hassan replied. "Let the boy take you back to his father, Mohammed the bird seller. There you can eat and make ready."

27

MOHAMMED, who was also a Sufi of the Mevlevi Order, led Georgiou through the streets to the *sema* hall that evening. They stopped outside a high, walled garden in the old part of the city and Mohammed knocked on a thick wooden door. It was opened by a short, bearded man wearing a green fez who greeted them with a slight bow, right arm folded across his heart.

In the middle of the garden was an old timber house. The front door opened onto a large room with an old stove in the middle and a marble fountain in one corner. Georgiou paused for an instant to admire the fine calligraphy around the walls.

"Those are the ninety-nine names of God," Mohammed explained. "For us, the greatest devotion, the greatest beauty, is the work of God in having made this world. We try to honor his example with our art.

"This is the house of our sheikh," Mohammed continued, as he led Georgiou up some old wooden steps to the *sema* hall on the second floor. "It has served as a meeting place for the

Sufis for more than three hundred years. His family has provided the sheikhs of our order for generations."

When they reached the *sema* hall, Georgiou realized that it was the place where the Sufis danced. Fifty or so men were already there. They were wearing long white skirts and tall felt hats. Some of them were turning slowly on the pivot of their left foot, counterclockwise, their arms crossed over their chests, their heads bowed. Musicians were gathering at one end of the hall. The walls were hung with fine Ottoman rugs. At the far end was a large inscription in Arabic over a regal chair. On the chair sat a man in dark robes and a turban. Georgiou gazed at him. It was Hassan Shushud.

Mohammed motioned to Georgiou to sit at the side with a few other young men and a couple of women. Mohammed unrolled his oud from its cover of green silk and joined the musicians. In a few moments they started playing, and a long, infinitely sweet, sad sound floated over the air; the sadness of a lover too long on his own.

The men in the felt hats and white skirts formed a long line, and one by one they shuffled, heads bowed, arms crossed over their chests, to the chair where Hassan was sitting. They bowed low before him, then turned to bow to another man in a white hat, the dance master, who was standing quietly, solemnly, in the middle of the hall. Slowly they began to turn, their left foot for an axis, their eyes closed. As they spun, their arms opened wide, the right palm offering itself to the heavens, the left facing down to earth.

Their heads gently inclined to the left, the dancers spun round and round the room, faster and faster, the music lifting their bodies as if they were dancing on air. The man in the white hat walked slowly among them, gently touching one here, another there. Like angels they spun, with not even one of them so much as brushing the other. One of the dancers was a boy of no more than eight or nine years. Another could have been in his eighties.

The look on their faces Georgiou had seen only once before: on the faces of the disciples in Fra Angelico's fresco in the Museo San Marco. Something of the same astonishment Georgiou had felt then came over him now. He was almost in a swoon. Though his eyes were open, there was no trace of movement in his mind. Almost imperceptibly, Hassan Shushud glanced over at the young man. A faint hint of a smile flickered in the dervish's eyes.

After what might have been hours—though who could tell?—the music rising to a pitch, falling again, and rising again, the dancers eventually peeled off one by one, bowed low to the dance master in the white hat, bowed low to their sheikh, Hassan Shushud, and returned to a single file along one side of the room. The music ebbed away, the hall returned to silence.

"I want to dance," Georgiou murmured, when his mind was able to find words. "I want to turn with the dervishes."

28

THE NEXT MORNING, over strong mint tea, Mohammed offered to let Georgiou live in his house and earn a small wage in his shop until he had enough money to continue his journey. Mohammed said he would be glad of the help, for his shop was busy. It was a custom of the Turkic peoples to keep caged songbirds and talking birds in their houses. It was said that the birds, especially the yellow canaries, brought the angels near.

Georgiou gladly accepted. Although he knew he could still find a painting commission should he need to—for there was an important Greek community in Istanbul—the shop would be a gateway into a Muslim world that he sensed had much to teach him. So Georgiou started selling songbirds on the main street that ran along the edge of the *soukh*. He learned to tell one bird from another, to gauge their state of health, their song, the quality of their plumage. The young Greek enjoyed his work, and business began to increase. Mohammed, pleased, quickly increased Georgiou's wages.

29

FOR SOME WEEKS Georgiou went every Friday to the *sema* with Mohammed, sitting in attendance as he had done that first evening. Each time he went, he was entranced. One evening, as the dervishes were departing, Hassan Shushud came over to him.

"I see that you are drawn to the path of love," he said.

Georgiou had no words for an answer.

"On Wednesdays and Sundays we teach the *sema* to those whose hearts wish for it. You may come on Sunday."

Hassan spoke with an unusual authority. He sounded different from the man Georgiou had met at his stall in the *soukh*. Georgiou gave a nod; it was almost a bow.

Two days later, Georgiou gathered with four other young men at the *sema* hall. For two hours the dance master showed them how to bring their attention down into the chest by following the breath. He called it bringing the mind down into the heart. Everything that turns needs an axis, he said—a spinning top, the earth, even a galaxy. The dervish needs an axis, a still center, too. For the dervish, the axis was his devotion, anchored in the heart. Without devotion, the dance master said, the dance was an empty performance that would serve no one. Georgiou thought of Father Dimitri; how he, too, had spoken of bringing the mind to the heart.

Slowly, over the following weeks, the young men were shown how to turn on themselves, the left foot remaining in contact with the floor, the right foot alternately raised at the knee and briefly in touch with the ground to give the spinner his motion. At first, they could spin for only a few moments before feeling dizzy or sick. It was a matter of attention, the dance master told them. The more deeply the mind fell into the heart, the less the body was disturbed by the motion.

When they had begun to master the mechanics of the movement, the dance master brought the musicians in. It was then that Georgiou began to understand what the dance master meant. The music drew his attention down into his body, away from the mind and its concerns about getting it right or wrong. He felt a softness, a warmth in the chest, and the more he let his body be moved by the music, the deeper the sensation in his chest became. As the weeks went on, he came to know what it was to have an inner attentiveness that seemed to fill his body with light so that he felt like he was dancing on air.

30

AS TIME PASSED, Georgiou began to learn the Turkish language. He had long conversations with Mohammed, and sometimes with Hassan Shushud, about the way of the dervishes. They told him how they had entered the order through their fathers, and that their families had been Mevlevis for generations.

Hassan Shushud, Mohammed told him, was known as a great master by the Sufis of Istanbul. He was a sheikh not only of the Mevlevi Order, but of the Bektashi and Helveti as well. As a young man, he had spent several years in the house of his master, barely going out, dwelling mostly in silence, absorbed in lengthy retreats. He had been blessed with many visions and graces from the invisible worlds. It was said that he could see into a person's soul and could tell one's future. He had a spiritual power—the Sufis called it *baraka*—that could sweep away the obstacles to spiritual progress in a disciple's mind. He exuded a sweetness that brought peace to all in his presence.

"Why does such a man have to sell flutes in the bazaar?" Georgiou asked Mohammed after dinner one evening.

"Work is a blessing for the Sufis," Mohammed replied. "First, it keeps us in humility, the greatest of all the virtues. It reminds us that we are like all other men. Work binds us to the common lot, and for that we are grateful. Then, work can bring heaven and earth together, through the attention we have toward it. When we fashion a flute or handle a bird with presence of mind, something is added to God's creation. Matter is raised up, ennobled by the attention we give it. In that way, we become cocreators with God of the material world; we raise both it and ourselves into the domain of spirit, which some also call love. That is why Hassan Shushud will be making flutes until the day he dies. He loves this mortal world with the same love he has for the invisible realms."

"And you, Mohammed, and Hassan, and the others, you all have wives. Most of you have families. Are not the cares and responsibilities of family life a distraction from your spiritual endeavors?"

Mohammed smiled at the young man's question.

"We Sufis have no monasteries," he replied. "For us, daily life itself is sacred. Every level of reality has its place, and it must be honored and given respect. All is God and of God. Daily life is a spiritual devotion, if you have this orientation of mind. As the head of a family, it is my joy to serve those in my care. It is an expression of my spiritual devotion as much as playing the oud in the *sema.* Only the form is different; the spirit, by God's grace, is the same."

Later the same evening, Georgiou pondered Mohammed's words alone in his room. He thought of Andros, in Florence, and even of Dimitri on Athos; how they, too, in their own ways, lived in the spirit that Mohammed had spoken of; from their deepest truth rather than from any prescribed rule. That night, as every night, Georgiou took the icon of the Blessed Virgin from his satchel and sat there with it by the light of a candle. He listened deeply for a long time. Before falling asleep, he knew that he would take the Virgin to Hassan Shushud.

31

WHEN HE FINISHED work the next evening, Georgiou took his satchel and walked through the streets to Hassan Shushud's house. He knocked on the garden gate, and Hassan's attendant, the man with the green fez, let him in. As he approached the timber house, Georgiou could hear the voices of men chanting softly.

A few Sufis were sitting around Hassan, and Georgiou quietly joined them on the floor. When the singing slowly ebbed away, Hassan picked up a book, kissed the cover, and read a line from it.

Love gives away every gift God bestows.

Hassan held Georgiou firmly in his gaze as he spoke the line. Georgiou sat there for a moment in silence. Then he undid his satchel and carefully unwrapped the icon of the Blessed Dark Mother from its protecting veil. The men in the room leaned forward. As they gazed upon it, a small tear began to form in the corner of the Mother's eye. The sheikh murmured a prayer, and the others joined him. The lights went dim, the men pressed their foreheads to the floor. Georgiou felt a warmth pass over his chest like a flame. At the same moment he heard a sound inside him, a long, drawn-out, single note, like the vibration from the string of a great harp.

"For a hundred years, since the time of my grandfather, we have been told to pray for this day," said Hassan. "My grandfather, who was the sheikh of our order in his time, had a dream that our lineage would die out during my lifetime unless the house were blessed by a tear from the Christian Virgin. For three hundred years, the line of our sheikhs has been unbroken. My wife has borne no children, but with the Our Lady's help, she will do so now."

Hassan leaned across to Georgiou and picked up the icon. He held it in front of his face for a few moments, his head bowed. Then he handed it back to the young man and lit a tall white candle in gratitude.

"This dark Virgin is not mine to keep," he said. "It is enough that you have brought Her into my presence. She already belongs to someone else. Keep Her safe, Georgiou, until you find her true home."

32

THE WEEKS TURNED into months. Georgiou almost forgot the world beyond Istanbul. Every now and then he would think of the road to Konya, how his journey was still unfinished; he would think of his father and Andros in Florence and send them a greeting with the wind. But for the most part he was absorbed in his new world, a world of dancing dervishes and songbirds, so that the world beyond the view of the minarets of the Blue Mosque seemed little more than a dream.

Hassan Shushud was keenly aware of the ease with which Georgiou had adopted their devotions. He watched over the young man's progress, and would summon him at times to his house. Sometimes they sat in silence, and when they did, Georgiou would hear things that he had never heard before. Once, he could have sworn that a voice cried out loud and filled the room with the name *Allah! Allah!* He glanced at Hassan, but the sheikh sat there sipping his glass of tea as if nothing had happened. Another time, he was certain he could hear the sweet sound of singing, but the windows were closed and there were only the two of them in the house.

Sometimes Hassan would ask Georgiou if he had any questions. Often Georgiou had none, and the silence would resume. He had come to love it so that to disturb it with words seemed clumsy. Occasionally he would wonder whether he was slipping into idleness; whether he ought to be doing or saying something. One day he mentioned this feeling to Hassan.

"People often take what they do to be the measure of who they are," Hassan Shushud said in reply. "If they are not doing something, either inwardly or outwardly, then they lose touch with the feeling of their existence. They get anxious, as if the gap in the action signified a gap in themselves. So people try to fill the hole in themselves with words and with doings of all kinds. Nobody wants to feel they are nobody.

"For the Sufis," Hassan continued, "silence is bliss. It is bliss because it gives room for the sensation of Being. Being is who we truly are, so when it arises, we feel a relief, a rest, a deep belonging. When you rest in Being, with the mind in the heart, you rest in the truth."

"It seems easier for me to fall into silence when I am with you," Georgiou said. "Why is that, Hassan? Is the Being you speak of contagious in some way?"

Hassan Shushud smiled.

"In a way, it is," he said. "As you know, Georgiou, we Sufis call it *baraka,* though you might also call it presence. Some people, either through grace or merit, are heavier with presence than others. It spreads out from them like a wave and nourishes those who are sensitive to it. They feel a stillness in that person's presence. The more you have the taste of this presence, the more you wish to rest in it. The more you rest there, the more you impart it to others, and without doing anything.

"Presence of this kind is another name for love," the sheikh continued. "Recite for me again the last line of your favorite poem."

Straw trembles in the presence of amber,

Georgiou murmured.

"Yes, that trembling is the connection," Hassan said. "The straw does not merge with the amber, nor the amber with the straw. In truth, they become even more themselves in the other's company. To become yourself is to invoke the presence of love. Sometimes it is visible as a trembling. Its presence is a third thing, felt in both lover and beloved, yet belonging to neither. It is not confined to any form, but it needs form to embody it."

Hassan paused for a moment and let his eyes take in the intricate pattern in the carpet on which they were sitting. Then, raising his head to look at Georgiou again, he continued.

"The form can be anything—a painting, the sound of the flute, the line of a poem, a leaf on a tree, another human being. Because we do not know what else to say, we mutter something about recognition. The other seems indescribably familiar to us. Being recognizes Being. That is what happened to Rumi when he met Shams. When this love arises between human beings, it is a special gift. It is both intimately personal and yet entirely beyond the person at the same time."

"I have known that love," Georgiou said, looking away through the window. "But my deepest prayer is that I may live it someday."

"Would you give your life?" Hassan asked. "Would you cut off your head and sit on it?"

Georgiou's attention snapped sharply back into the room. The sheikh had just used the same words as Sofroniou, the hermit on Athos. Georgiou did not reply, though his mouth was open.

33

WHEN HE WAS not with the dervishes, Georgiou was busy with his customers in Mohammed's shop. One day, a man walked in who—Georgiou could tell from his gestures and mannerisms—was from Italy. He wanted to buy a white cockatoo in a gilded cage for his wife.

"She is back in Florence," the man said to Georgiou. "I have been in Istanbul on business for weeks now, but I am leaving for home tomorrow. I shall be glad to be back in the civilized air of my own city again, after the dust and the noise of Istanbul."

In Italian, Georgiou told the man that he, too, was from Florence, and that he had been away for many months now. Then, as if remembering something himself, he said he was on his way to Konya, and only then would he be returning to Italy. When the man asked what his occupation in Florence was, Georgiou told him of his father and how he had followed in his footsteps.

"Then what is it that takes you so far away from our beautiful city?" the stranger asked.

"You would seem to have all you need there, a fine profession and a warm home."

"Love has taken me away," Georgiou replied, surprised at his own frankness to a stranger. "Though for what or for whom I still do not know."

"Ah, but of course, what else?" the Italian smiled. "We Italians are all smitten with the same passion."

"No, you do not understand," Georgiou tried to explain. "I am Greek, not Italian, and I am not sure that my love is entirely of this world."

"There is no love that is not of this world," the Italian laughed. "Even our priests know that. The only reason we are here is to love."

Georgiou had no answer to that. The Florentine picked out his cockatoo in its gilded cage and bade the young man farewell. But his visit had stirred something in Georgiou. He began having thoughts of Florence again, and of Konya, how he had still not gotten to the end of the road.

34

IN THE BRIEF hours of his free time Georgiou would visit old Istanbul—the early Byzantine churches, the cobbled streets behind the Topkapi Palace, the open markets that ran along the edge of the *soukh*. He rode the ferries on the Bosphorus for the sheer pleasure of watching the coasts of Europe and Asia glide past him. He spent precious afternoons gazing at the mosaics in Hagia Sophia, which means Holy Wisdom, the greatest cathedral of Byzantium and the one that the Sultan Mehmet had converted into the Blue Mosque.

It had been a Tuesday, on a late May afternoon in 1453, when the sultan entered the vanquished city, known then as Constantinople. He rode directly to Hagia Sophia and was so humbled by its beauty that he had it turned into the imperial mosque.

The week after the Italian's visit to Mohammed's shop, Georgiou went to Hagia Sophia with Hassan Shushud. Hassan showed him a mosaic he had not noticed before. It was in a small cupola off to one side of the main cathedral. The two men stood for a few moments before a scene in which one bird was drinking at a fountain while another looked on. The birds were in gold against a background of deep Byzantine blue.

"This scene means a lot to the Sufis," Hassan said.

Georgiou looked at him, perplexed.

"The early Christians made this image," Hassan continued, "but a mystic of any religion will sense its meaning. Do you see how one part of us, the personality, goes about its daily business of eating and drinking, while another part, the soul, watches over it all the while? These two birds are companions. We do not have to choose between the one and the other. We need them both, for together they make us human. If we were just one, we would be lost in the daily round of appetites and desires. If we were the other only, we would be with the angels, not here on earth."

"It seems to me that most of us are lost in our appetites," Georgiou responded. "Does that mean that the other bird can fall asleep?"

"The other bird is asleep until it hears a call," Hassan replied. "We need to listen for that call. It is ever present, but some people are never silent enough to hear it. Then there are those—

and you are among them, Georgiou—in whom the second bird is sometimes awake and sometimes asleep. It is in these people that the longing for a nameless something rubs away at their heart. These people are called, but by what, they cannot say."

"A man came into the shop a few days ago who said that there can be no love that is not of this world. What do you say to this, Hassan?"

"The man is right, Georgiou, for we only see the presence of love when it touches someone or something in this world—the straw and the amber, remember. Yet the man is also wrong, for the source of love is beyond the stars. It can never be pointed to, even though it makes everything in its orbit shine. Let the one bird feed while the other watches over, Georgiou. Then a door may open, and love may swoop down in the middle of the night, when you are least ready for it, and steal your heart forever."

Hassan Shushud led the young man to a stone bench outside the cupola.

"I sense that the thought of your journey has been kindled again in your heart," he said, when they had sat down. "Your stay in Istanbul has prepared you for the way. It is time for you to move on. Times are changing, Georgiou, and the way of the Sufis is changing, too. There are Sufis who are invisible today; Sufis who do not wear robes, who do not take part in the ancient ceremonies, and who do not even call themselves Sufis.

"Their path leads them ever more into the world," Hassan continued, "not away from it. They can be found in all walks of life. They may be captains of industry, housewives, even lawyers. Yet while engaged in their work, a part of them looks quietly on, like the bird. This is your path, and your riddle to solve, too, Georgiou."

"I have been shown a truth and beauty by your hands that would silence both worlds," Georgiou answered. "My mind is quieter than I have ever known, my days are more content than all the days I have ever lived. Yet something tells me I must go on my way. Life has become more of a mystery than I could have ever dreamed of."

"Life is always a mystery, Georgiou," Hassan murmured. "The more we think we know where we are going, the less we are joined to the way of things. Your story is calling you. Listen for it, and watch, like the bird."

Georgiou bowed low and kissed his sheikh's hand.

As Hassan stood up to leave, he handed a letter to Georgiou.

"Take this to the person in Konya whose address is on the envelope. Her name is Sophia

Sarmoun. She is not of our order, or of any order other than her own. She moves with the wind, though I hear she is in Konya now. She will know more about your journey than you do yourself. She knows more about everything than anyone I know. And be prepared. Whatever happens, it will not be what you expect."

Hassan put his arm on Georgiou's shoulder. "I have one last piece of news. My wife is expecting our baby," he smiled, kissing Georgiou farewell on both cheeks.

35

GEORGIOU was sad to leave his friends in Istanbul, but Hassan was right; when it is time to move on, even the stars lend their will to the change. Mohammed's eldest son, Ali, had returned from Persia, where he had been on a buying expedition for more birds. Now that he was home, Mohammed had less need of Georgiou's help in the shop. Georgiou had earned enough to continue his journey, so two days after his meeting with Hassan, and too eager to arrive finally to be content with walking, he boarded the early-morning bus for Konya.

He sat at the back of the crowded bus with his satchel clutched in his arms. How strange, after all this time on the journey, he thought, the streets of Istanbul gliding by, to know that before the day was out he would finally step off the bus in Konya.

Along a lake of long shadows and rose sky they drove, then across a great empty plain and on into the dusty wilderness of Anatolia where long ago the Christians of Byzantium had scraped their homes and churches out of the high limestone rocks. Once, to settle the dust and soothe the throat, the ticket collector lurched through the bus and sprinkled everyone with rosewater. Finally the minarets of Konya rose on the horizon, the green domes of the city's mosques glinting in the last rays of sun.

Georgiou stepped into the main street and eagerly looked about him. Konya seemed no different from any other city he had passed through in Turkey. Long dusty streets and winding alleys, carpet sellers haggling with customers, the muezzin calling the faithful to prayer, the cafés with the men huddling over water pipes. All his wanderings and meetings and adventures had led to this place. He had been brought to Konya by a feeling he was unable to deny. But now that he was here, what was he meant to do?

There was only one thing to do. He asked one of the men in a café for directions to the tomb of Jelaluddin Rumi. Then, his heart beating like a drum, he ran, then walked, then ran again down the street to the shrine of the saint. On the way he bought a pair of red roses.

He came at last to a high white wall with an arch in the middle. Georgiou passed through the arch and entered a courtyard cooled by the waters of a large marble fountain. A conical dome of shimmering green tiles formed the roof of the mausoleum. At the pinnacle was a golden crescent moon and star. By its side a slim minaret soared to the sky. People were strolling in and out of the mausoleum, children were trailing their hands in the fountain, families gathered quietly in corners.

Georgiou entered through the great iron doors, and there before him were the tombs of those saints who had followed after Rumi, the sheikhs of the Mevlevi Order of Whirling Dervishes. On each tomb stood the tall hat of the sheikh whose body lay below. The hats were wound in long white cloth, and around them were inscribed the names of God, the Almighty, the All Compassionate, the All Merciful.

Georgiou made his way through the silent room to the far end and came to a standstill before the tomb of Rumi. Here lay the man who had written those words, "All the particles of the world are in love and looking for lovers." This was the man who had inspired thousands through the centuries and to this very day to give their all for a love that has no name.

Georgiou placed his roses on the tomb, then knelt down in silence. He felt at first a deep contentment, like the relief of arriving home. Then, the peace in his heart began to change into a sweet but painful sadness. It was as if the unshed tears of a lifetime had all welled up at once.

For an hour or more he remained there, bereft of something, though he didn't know what; humbled, yet grateful, so grateful, for this deep cleft in his heart that joined him somehow to every other human being, to every suffering soul. How fortunate he was, he felt, to know this deep sorrow that spread out from his heart and washed over him, a softening wave.

36

THE NEXT DAY Georgiou went to the address that Hassan had given him. He knocked loud and long on the stout wooden door, but no one came to open it. The next morning the same thing happened, as it did the morning after that. Georgiou persisted—each morning an unanswered knock, then the rest of the day in the shrine of Jelaluddin Rumi, sitting in the silence before his tomb, oblivious of the comings and goings of the pilgrims.

Sometimes, memories from his very first years would float through his mind: moments of tenderness with his mother, of crying through the night in her absence; and of being alone with his father in a foreign world.

Often he would rest, content, aware only of the silence that hums through the days, obscured so often beneath hopes and cares. As he sat by the tomb, all the questions Georgiou had had about his life and his journey—and about love—began to disappear. It no longer seemed to matter why he was in Konya, or what direction his life should take on his return to Florence.

Then one morning, as he walked toward Rumi's shrine, his feet seemed to refuse to follow their usual course. Georgiou paused. A dove fluttered by and drifted down a street to his left. He turned and followed it. The dove flew just ahead of him, landing finally on the domed roof of a small stone building with an open door. Georgiou looked at the sign on the wall. It was the shrine dedicated to Shams, the man who had opened wide the gates of love in Rumi's heart. The traveler stepped inside.

The shrine was much smaller and humbler than Rumi's, and not many pilgrims went there. The tomb was draped in a large green cloth of silk and brocade. A small dervish's hat had been placed at one end of it. A taper burned in a glass bowl of oil suspended from the ceiling by three silver chains.

A lone figure was kneeling in front of the tomb. Georgiou saw that it was a woman. She wore a scarf over her head, and though he could not see her features he was immediately aware of the strength of her presence.

As he came up behind her, he was aware of a power in her that seemed to emanate from her body like light rays. Georgiou's thoughts evaporated. He felt himself drawn into a field so strong that it brought him to his knees beside her. A silence filled not only his mind but every corner of the shrine. It was so deep that not a muscle in Georgiou's body moved. The woman remained motionless beside him.

Then, as if from a deep well, she spoke:

"I am not the One you are looking for," she said. "I am not that One. But I am no different from her. Follow me."

"Who are you?" Georgiou was filled with awe. He could barely get the question out of his mouth, but the woman did not answer him. She rose to her feet, and with a low bow to the tomb of Shams, she slowly backed her way out into the street. Georgiou scrambled to his feet and followed her.

37

HE HURRIED after her through the streets to a quarter that by now had become all too familiar to him. Finally, she stopped at the wooden door he had been hammering on each morning for several days. Unlocking it, the woman gestured for Georgiou to follow her. She went up a steep flight of stairs and ushered Georgiou into a large room whose walls were draped with ancient tapestries. She sat on a long ottoman couch and motioned for him to sit beside her.

The woman took the scarf from her head, and Georgiou stared at her in disbelief. Her face was the face of his icon, only older. Her long dark hair was swept to one side and fastened with the same silver clasp. Her large charcoal eyes gazed at him, fathomless and serene.

"I knocked on your door again and again." Georgiou fumbled for words. "But no one ever responded."

"You were not ready." The woman smiled softly.

"Who are you? What do you want of me?"

Georgiou could barely get the words out of his mouth.

"I want nothing," the woman replied. "I am no more than a mirror, Georgiou, held up to your eyes. When you are ready to know this, return to me here. Your knock will be answered. But when you return, know that you must give yourself into my charge for a time that will be as long as it is long."

Georgiou's whole journey swam before his eyes. He saw all the times when strange synchronicities, even miracles, had helped him on his way. Sitting there on the woman's ottoman, he knew more clearly than at any time before that his life was not in his hands—and that it never had been. He could never have dreamed up the moment he found himself in now. It was as if everything he had lived through, all the help, seen and unseen, that he had received along the way, had converged into this one moment. There was nothing to do but to trust it. He felt a deep reverence for this woman whose image he had been painting without knowing it. Finally, he spoke.

"I am ready now," he said.

38

SOPHIA SARMOUN stood up, fetched a silver bowl of water, and placed it on the table before Georgiou. She took a small bottle of rosewater and shook a few drops into the bowl. Then she lit a tall white candle in the corner of the room.

"This candle will continue burning until we next meet," she said, sitting once more by Georgiou's side. "In your deepest moments of darkness, remember its flame."

She dipped her right hand in the silver bowl and sprinkled the rose-scented water over Georgiou's head.

"Now place your hands in the bowl. Let your hopes and fears be washed away. Place all your trust in the compassion of the Mother. Know, Georgiou, that whatever happens, you are under her protection."

She took a towel, dried Georgiou's hands, and held them for a few moments in hers. Georgiou felt her eyes reaching down into all the forgotten regions of his life. He knew that nothing was hidden from her.

"Follow me," she said. "Bring your satchel with you." She started down the stairs toward the front door but stopped at the bottom. There on the left, behind a thick curtain, was another door. Sophia Sarmoun pulled the curtain aside, unlocked the iron door, and ushered Georgiou down a few steps into a small room with no windows. The room was empty but for a bed, a tank of water with a pitcher beneath it, and a wooden table with a large bowl of fruit in the middle. A thick Turkish carpet lay on the floor by the bed. A small door opened onto a bathroom.

"Georgiou." The woman spoke his name firmly. "You will stay in this room until I come for you. You know in your heart already that there is nothing to fear. Everything you need shall come to you. Remember, all shall be well, Georgiou. All shall be well."

Then the woman closed the door and Georgiou found himself in pitch darkness. It was only then that he realized there were no lights in the room. He began to sweat, even though the room was cool. He groped his way to the bed and sat on it, his hands clammy still, his brow wet.

He tried to remember the practice that Dimitri, on Athos, and the Sufis in Istanbul had taught him. *Bring your mind down into your heart,* he said to himself. *Breathe into the heart.* He fumbled for his satchel, undid the straps, and held his icon tightly to his chest.

The darkness was so thick that there was not even a chink of light from the door. He tried to remember where the table was, and the door to the bathroom. He stood up, the Virgin at his chest still, and began to edge his way around the room, his free arm extended before him. He stumbled against the water tank. He opened the faucet at the bottom of the tank and, filling the pitcher with water, drank from it in gulps. Slowly, he felt his way back to the bed.

He sat there, quieter for a moment. There was no sound. He sniffed the air. It was faintly musty; he wrinkled his nose. He laid the icon by his side and sat back against the wall. All he could hear was the sound of his own breathing. He moved his arms around in front of him, trying to feel the texture of the dark. He was motionless for a while, until finally he started to feel drowsy.

He dozed in fits and starts, his back still against the wall. Suddenly he woke up and, disoriented, wondered where he was. He remembered. Was it morning or night? He had no idea. He felt a current of fear. How long was he going to be in this darkness? And why?

Georgiou reached for the icon, and felt a bead of moisture forming around her eye. He felt his breathing drop down into his heart. His fear ebbed away. He remembered what he had said to Sophia Sarmoun, that he was ready for whatever came next. It was true, he thought. *There is nothing left for me to do but trust; to trust this woman, the way I was brought to her, and this darkness that surrounds me now.*

39

GEORGIOU slept long and often, especially in the beginning. But whenever he awoke, it was always to darkness. With no alternation of day and night, he lost all sense of time. When he was awake, the darkness enveloped him like a velvet blanket. It swallowed his thoughts and returned them to the silence that filled the room. His mind slowed almost to a standstill. Every now and then a flash of fear would crackle through his body like lightning, jerking him alive.

Then he would take the Dark Mother and hold her to his breast, praying for her protection. When he felt a tear beginning to form on her eye, he would feel quiet, and he would remember, "All shall be well."

Just when the dark was beginning to feel safe and familiar to him, Georgiou began to see things. At first, the darkness seemed to turn gray. Then little sparks of light danced before his eyes. He began to see scenes from his life light up in the darkness, as if on a cinema screen. He saw himself in the museum, before the fresco of the Sermon on the Mount; he saw his father teaching him to paint. He saw himself as a child standing alone and bewildered in a deserted street. He saw his mother lying sick in a bed, and his father crying beside her. He saw hundreds of people on a station platform, all scrambling and screaming to board a train that would never fit them all in.

He saw fleeting shapes that came and went, strange creatures made of light that disappeared before they had fully formed. At first, these apparitions frightened him. Then, as he became more accustomed to them, Georgiou found himself watching them, and himself, like the bird at the fountain in the mosaic in Hagia Sophia. He was a witness, not only to the events of his life, but also to his participation in them. He began to discover a part of himself that, no matter what happened, remained forever untouched and at peace.

As a witness to his own life, Georgiou was able to see down into the roots of his fears, into the source of his boredom, his restlessness, his apathy. All these moods and more would wash over him in the dark. He saw how his mind sought refuge in memories of the past, and in hopes for the future.

He came to see each eddy in his mind as if it were passing by in slow motion. He was able to see the way his thoughts spawned more thoughts; how they perpetually ran after each other. Every movement of his body and mind slowed to the pace of a diver in deep water. Gradually, he began to lose his ordinary awareness of his body. Without the sight of it, and without any reference in time, he could no longer locate himself. His limbs felt spongy, weightless. The only part of him that remained was his breath.

Eventually, the only sense that was alive in him was a simple quiet that lay like bedrock beneath all his hopes and fears. That quiet was Georgiou's refuge. It was always there, whether he was awake or asleep, neither beginning nor fading away.

Once, into that quiet, the presence of his mother came. He didn't see her but he could feel her by his side, so clearly that in that instant Georgiou knew that death itself was a lie. His heart was filled with joy, for he knew then that all was well with her, and that she had always been with him.

40

FOR DAYS ON END Georgiou remained in the quiet, with little sense of his body and rarely a thought in his mind.

Then, just as he was on the edge of sleep, a wild-eyed woman suddenly burst out of the dark and filled the whole room in a frenzied dance, brandishing a long knife in each of her arms. Her naked body was blood red, her hair a tangle of writhing black snakes. Two more snakes wound about her waist, fangs flicking like lightning. A necklace of human skulls rattled around her throat. Her two eyes flashed like rainbows; her third eye, in the center of her forehead, was a bloodshot ring of fire.

Georgiou froze. For a moment, fear was all he was. Then he stepped back behind his fear and was able to watch it all happen in awe. The dreadful form danced in a fury before him, then suddenly lunged and swung her knives in the direction of Georgiou's neck. In that instant, Georgiou felt his whole life story—his work as an icon painter, his journeying, his romance with the poetry of Rumi, his restlessness, his wondering, his thirst for the new—all of it falling away. He watched in amazement as his head, sliced from his neck, seemed to drop to the floor and roll toward the wild dancing woman. She grabbed it by the hair, laughed the most terrible laugh, swung it round and round, and dissolved with it into the darkness.

Only the ring of fire, her third eye, remained and continued to glow on its own. Georgiou stared at it. Slowly, it began to expand into the shimmering vision of a woman's face. She was as beautiful as the dancing woman had been terrible. She smiled a radiant smile and gazed at him with warm blue eyes that filled the darkness with light. Her golden hair fell to her shoulders; her skin, smooth as a young girl's, was creamy white. Her face was ensconced in a white scallop shell.

Gradually, the woman's face dissolved back into the ring of fire, which in turn was swallowed up by the dark.

41

GEORGIOU no longer cared how long he would spend alone in the darkness. He knew now that both the dark and the light arise and return to that same stillness. Knowing that his imperfections had their place in the scheme of things in the same way his gifts and talents did, he felt compassion for himself and his failings. There was nothing to change in the way he was. There was nothing in this world or the next to fear. No harm could come.

It was into that quiet that, suddenly, the tiniest chink of daylight came. Georgiou clapped his hand to his eyes and, looking between his fingers, turned to see where it came from. There seemed to be a tiny hole that had opened in the door to the room.

"Do not move." It was the voice of Sophia Sarmoun. "Let your eyes accustom themselves to the light."

In a while, Sophia opened the door just a crack. Then gradually, inch by inch, she opened the door wider. When Georgiou was finally able to see her full form in the hallway beyond, it wasn't what he could see that astonished him; it was the sheer fact of light, marvelous beyond belief. What he had taken for granted all his life now seemed a miracle. Everything, even Sophia's form, was light, dancing and pulsing.

Blinking and rubbing his eyes, Georgiou stumbled toward her and fell at her feet. "Thank you," he whispered, his voice hoarse from disuse. "Thank you. You have allowed me to see what my eyes could not see. You have caused me to know what my mind could never know."

42

"COME," Sophia said, as she turned to go up the stairs. Georgiou followed her, his steps uncertain, up to the room where he had first sat with her on the ottoman couch. She brought him a bowl of thick soup and a glass of tea, then watched him as he ate in silence.

When he had finished he sat there for a moment, as if deep in thought. He looked up at Sophia Sarmoun. Then he reached into his satchel and carefully drew out his icon of the Dark Mother.

"I want you to have this," he said, holding it toward her with both hands. "I know it is yours."

She leaned forward and took the icon from his hands.

"Thank you," she said, gazing at the Dark Virgin Mother. "It is I who belong to Her."

They sat there in silence for a while, Georgiou aware of the birds singing in her garden outside.

"I have no questions, nothing to say," he said finally.

Sophia nodded. "Yes, the seeker has fallen away," she said. "You have welcomed yourself home. But the feast has not yet begun. For that, you must go back to where you belong."

After a little while, and without further words, Sophia Sarmoun took Georgiou's hand. He bent to kiss her hand, and then he went down the stairs, out into the busy street.

43

GEORGIOU took the next bus back to Istanbul, where he boarded a ship for Italy. After five days of rough seas and high winds, Georgiou reached Brindisi once again, and after one more dusty bus ride, he finally caught sight of the red roof of the Duomo, gleaming in the Tuscan sun.

He walked across the Ponte Santa Trinita to the Church of Santa Croce and bowed his head once more before the statue of Dante, in gratitude for his safe return. He walked on to the Piazza San Marco and along the cobbled street that led to his house. Stefanou, his father, was by the door, watering the climbing roses, his old corduroy pants flecked with fresh paint from an icon. For a second, the two men stood still in the middle of the street. Then, with a shout, they clasped each other in their arms, both of them weeping with joy.

That night they went to visit Andros, and the three of them stayed up into the small hours so that Georgiou could share all his stories. Andros could feel a contentment in Georgiou that he himself had only come to know in his later years. *He has become a man,* Andros thought to himself, as he listened to Georgiou speaking. *He will no longer be driven; he is the driver now.*

Georgiou settled into the Florentine rhythm with an ease that surprised everyone but him. He took up his work again and was at peace in it. Once again, he began to spend his leisure time in the museums and churches—simply for the beauty to be found there. And sometimes, he would spend an hour on the *terrazza* of the Caffè Bergelli, on the Piazza of the Blessed Annunciation. He would sip his cappuccino, watch the world go by, and admire the graceful arches of the Colonnade of the Innocents and the beauty of the Florentine women.

44

A FEW WEEKS after his return, Georgiou was standing in front of Botticelli's masterpiece *The Birth of Venus* in the Uffizi Gallery, the greatest museum in Florence. He had come early, when they were opening the doors, to avoid the throngs of tourists.

Georgiou loved this painting. Cheap reproductions of it were on sale all over the world, yet the power and beauty of the original always astounded him. He loved the way Botticelli brought the mystery of beauty into being. In a single female form, Venus rising from the ocean in a scallop shell, he had unified the sensuous goddess of love with the divine tenderness of the Virgin Mary.

Georgiou drew closer to the painting, marveling at the luminous subtleties of color; the greens and blues of ocean and sky, the rich red of the cloak held out to cover the goddess, the delicate pink of the roses fluttering in the wind.

Absorbed in the Botticelli, he never stirred when a young woman came into the gallery and stood behind him. Flora, too, had come to look at *The Birth of Venus,* as she had done often since arriving in Florence to study art, already more than two years before. She had been there for some moments when the young man in front of her turned, as if to leave. Her eyes met his, and in that moment the whole arc of her life fell into place. She knew this man. She had known him forever. How strangely natural, ordinary even, to be standing before him now. Her face broke into a broad, open smile.

Georgiou, aware of someone there as he turned to go, found his glance returned by a tall, erect woman, a foreigner. They both smiled. Neither of them spoke. Her fine chiseled bones and wide-open eyes were framed by her long fair hair. Her gaze showered him with a direct, uncomplicated warmth, as if she were welcoming a dear friend. He felt this same warmth pour through his body; an indescribable feeling of home.

Who are you? The thought passed through his mind without forming into words. But as soon as the question came, the woman spoke, still smiling.

"Haven't you recognized me yet?" she murmured.

Flora spoke with a simple authority, her Italian vowels shaped by an American twang. All her life, even as a child in Indiana, she had known that she was loved by an invisible love.

She felt the presence of this intimacy and conversed with it, whenever she was on her own. That presence had always been enough for her, her own private consolation and joy. Yet when her eyes met Georgiou's, she knew that she had found the expression of this love in form.

Georgiou's mouth dropped open. His whole body flushed. Even as her words ebbed away, the question still echoing on in his mind, he suddenly knew the answer.

Her face was the one he had seen in his vision in the dark room.

The same generous eyes pouring with radiance; the same open smile. The woman who had burst out of the dark was beaming at him now in person, in a long floral skirt and a white blouse tied at the waist. And they had met by the painting of a woman in a scallop shell!

She was literally a dream come true. In that first shock of recognition, Georgiou felt the secret gate in his heart spring open; the gate that allows someone to love another human being completely; and through that devotion, to know a love for all things, great and small, under the sun. Standing there before her, in awe of the workings of his own destiny, his inner being began to bow, even while not knowing to what.

That morning, in the Uffizi Gallery in Florence, Georgiou had finally discovered Rumi's secret for himself: there is only love, and, by grace, one love can take you home. In loving another utterly—whether it be Christ, or Shams, the love of your life, even an open flower—if every last cell in you is carried away, then nothing is left out and the earth and the sky become one.

So it was that Georgiou's faith in a love he could not name, and Flora's faith in a love she could not see, brought them together under the gaze of Botticelli's Venus. The strange thing was, Georgiou would think for years afterward, when they were married, it was as if the whole story had been written from the very beginning. And, of course, it probably was.

ABOUT THE AUTHOR

Roger Housden is the author of several books of nonfiction, including *Sacred America* (Simon & Schuster, 1999), and his new best-selling book, *Ten Poems to Change Your Life* (Harmony, 2001). This is his first novel. A native of Bath, England, Housden moved to the United States in 1998. He now lives in Woodstock, New York, with his wife, Marion. You can contact him by email at chasingrumi@juno.com